THE HAUNTED GALLERY

Baffling robberies and mysterious murders are the stock-in-trade of Miss Victoria Lincoln, private detective . . . After Professor Marchant dies, his house, Bartley Towers, is visited nightly by a sinister enemy, which frequents the gallery containing the Professor's collection of antiques and curios. When the detective investigates the case, she calls on the assistance of Caroline Gerrard . . . Thereafter, Miss Lincoln and Miss Gerrard investigate a series of bizarre cases, which are seemingly insoluble . . . until Victoria Lincoln gets to work . . .

JOHN RUSSELL FEARN

$\blacklozenge$

THE HAUNTED GALLERY

EDITED BY PHILIP HARBOTTLE

Complete and Unabridged

LINFORD
Leicester

First published in Great Britain

First Linford Edition
published 2011

British Library CIP Data

Fearn, John Russell, *1908 – 1960.*
    The haunted gallery. - -
    (Linford mystery library)
    1. Women private investigators- -Fiction.
    2. Detective and mystery stories.
    3. Large type books.
    I. Title II. Series
    823.9′12–dc22

    ISBN 978–1–4448–0636–6

Published by
F. A. Thorpe (Publishing)
Anstey, Leicestershire

Set by Words & Graphics Ltd.
Anstey, Leicestershire
Printed and bound in Great Britain by
T. J. International Ltd., Padstow, Cornwall

This book is printed on acid-free paper

1

The Haunted Gallery

Over the lovely and historic old pile of Bartley Towers hung a cloak of sorrow, gloom and mystery. For its owner, the famous Professor Marchant, was dead; and in some inexplicable way a stealthy, sinister enemy who walked by night was gaining access to the gallery which housed the Professor's collection of antiques and curios. Night after night the same thing was happening. The gallery door would be securely locked when everyone retired to bed; but in the morning it would be open — and another valuable antique would be lying smashed to smithereens on the floor!

Dorothy Mannall, the late Professor's young secretary, was at her wit's end to know what to do; for she felt herself to be responsible for the safety of the collection.

One afternoon she spoke to Caroline

Gerrard about it. Carol was the Professor's niece. She'd been given a special holiday from Shelburne College to attend Professor Marchant's funeral and to be present at the reading of the will.

They sat in the dining room, gazing moodily out over the spacious, sunlit grounds. Dorothy cupped her chin in her hands and frowned.

'Carol, I've been thinking. When I was at Shelburne the head girl of the Sixth, and the school captain, was a marvellous girl named Victoria Lincoln. I bet you've heard of her — eh?'

Caroline nodded eagerly.

'I certainly have, Dot! She walked away with just about every prize there was. You can see her name on practically every plaque in the school hall.'

Dorothy said reminiscently:

'That's right, Carol. She won the Harmsworth Musical three years running . . . I've never heard anyone to equal her on the piano. She was no bookworm, though — she skippered the hockey and cricket elevens during her last three terms, and won the County women's mile open

2

championship twice. She could do any-thing in the swimming baths, and she was no duffer with a tennis racquet either. Then during her last term she won first prize in an all-England essay competition for schoolgirls, on the subject: *What I'd like to do when I leave school.'*

'Honestly?' breathed Carol, her eyes wide with excitement. 'Gosh — this Victoria Lincoln must've been a wonder woman! Well, go on, Dot . . . what was it she wanted to do when she left?'

Dorothy laughed.

'Trust Vicky to be different! She said she wanted to be a private detective!'

'What? A lady detective?'

'That's it; and what's more, she did it, too! Her folks were pretty wealthy and her Dad opened an office for her in Regent Street, in London. There was a big paragraph in the *Ashburton Times* about it. I remember Miss Booth reading it out to us one morning at breakfast, the term after Vicky had left.'

Carol squeezed Dorothy's arm. Her voice fairly trembled with eagerness.

'Oh, Dot — I'd give anything in the

world to meet Miss Lincoln! What does she look like?'

'Ah, she's beautiful, Carol . . . tall, slim — with soft, coal-black wavy hair, dark eyes always full of fun, a cute oval face and a skin like you see in the face-cream advertisements. Shelburne will never have another Vicky Lincoln . . . never!'

Suddenly Carol said:

'Listen, Dot — if she's a detective . . . why not call her in to help us with the mystery of Uncle's antiques being smashed?'

Dorothy smacked her hands together.

'Carol, you've had a real brainwave! You're dying to meet Vicky — and so you shall! I'll find her in the 'phone book and give her a ring right away. Why on earth didn't I think of it before?'

Thrilling with eager anticipation Caroline followed the young secretary to the 'phone.

★　★　★

Miss Victoria Lincoln smiled as she shook hands with Dorothy Mannall in the sunlit hall of Bartley Towers.

'I caught the very first train, Miss

Mannall! I was very interested in your message. You see, I conducted an enquiry once for the late professor Marchant. He was a most remarkable man!'

Dorothy had no thoughts just then for anyone save the heroine of her schooldays.

'Vicky! I mean — Miss Lincoln . . . oh, I don't suppose you remember me! I was in the Fourth when you were captain of Shelburne. We used to worship you from afar, sort of thing. You certainly were a goddess to us insignificant little shrimps!'

Miss Lincoln laughed, her white, even teeth flashing like pearls.

'Well, well! So we're old schoolmates, eh, Dorothy? You know, I *do* remember you vaguely. Didn't you skipper the second eleven netball team the year Shelburne won the Southern Counties Junior Cup?'

'That's right, Miss Lincoln!' Dorothy smiled gleefully. 'You must have a marvellous memory. I shouldn't have thought you'd have even known I was alive!'

'Ah, no, you're wrong, Dorothy. After all, it's not so very long ago, you know! Four or five years at most. I'm not an old woman yet by a long way. Now

. . . wouldn't you like to tell me about Professor Marchant?'

Dorothy Mannall nodded.

'I couldn't wish to work for anyone more understanding, or more generous, Miss Lincoln. He was such a kindly man — that's what makes all these dreadful things that have been happening since his death so inexplicable.'

'Yes — so I gathered from your message. I'd like to get to work right away, so if you'll give me the details . . . '

Over coffee in the lounge the Professor's young secretary gave the detective a few particulars.

'I'm in charge of the house, Miss Lincoln, until the will is read and the estate finally settled; so you can see why everyone blames *me* for what's been going on.'

'Everyone? You have guests, then, or . . . ?'

'Yes. Two life-long friends of the Professor; Harvey Benson and his sister Jane, and the Professor's niece, Caroline Gerrard. Then there's Roger Pell, the estate manager.'

'Anyone else?'

'No one that is, beside the servants.

There's only three, and they've been here practically all their lives. We can definitely rule them out, Miss Lincoln.'

'Right. Now try and give me a clear idea of what's been happening.'

'Well, it's all to do with Professor Marchant's collection of antiques. They're all kept in what's known as the Haunted Gallery. They . . . '

Victoria Lincoln raised her brows.

'I'd no idea Bartley Towers is supposed to be haunted?'

Dorothy laughed.

'You know how it is — the way these old country folk love their legends! Anyhow, the strangest things have been happening in that gallery. The Professor's lovely curios are being destroyed one by one, and I'm at my wit's end. I'm the only one who has a key to the door and the french windows at the other end always are kept locked. So . . . '

Victoria put down her cup, jumped up.

'Suppose we take a look at this gallery, Miss Mannall?'

The secretary nodded, produced a bunch of keys, led the way into the hall.

As they neared the stairs the front door opened and in strode a short, thick-set young fellow wearing rough tweeds. His cheery whistling stopped when he saw Miss Mannall and the young detective.

'Ah, there you are, Dot! Look, I've searched all over the grounds but there's no trace of any blinking burglar; and as for a ghost . . . well, I think Miss Benson's been dreaming.'

Miss Mannall did the introductions.

'This is Roger Pell, the estate manager. Roger, meet Miss Victoria Lincoln, the detective I was telling you about.'

'I'm really glad you've come to help us, ma'am,' declared Pell, shaking hands warmly. 'It's had us all beat, I'm afraid.'

'What were you saying about a ghost?' Victoria asked.

Roger Pell shrugged.

'Ah, I think it's an old wife's tale! It's Jane Benson, she's staying here — she reckons she saw a ghostly female form in white draperies, gliding along the terrace underneath her bedroom window last night. Personally I think the old girl's crazy. I . . . '

He broke off as a startled scream echoed out from somewhere above them. For a few seconds everyone stood motionless, listening. Then Miss Mannall grabbed the detective's arm.

'That yell came from the Haunted Gallery, Miss Lincoln! I'm sure of that . . . come on, let's go!'

As they started for the stairs Victoria said:

'I thought you said you always kept the door locked, Miss Mannall?'

'Yes — I do, always. Nevertheless, I'm sure that scream came from there. Anyway, we'll soon see.'

Roger Pell was ahead of them. When they reached the first landing he was standing outside a massive oak door, stamping about impatiently.

'Hurry, for Heaven's sake! Dot, I'm certain I can hear someone in there!'

Miss Mandall fumbled with her keys to find the right one. Next second Victoria Lincoln said drily:

'Don't bother, young lady — the door's unlocked!'

She threw it open as she spoke, the

9

other two crowding behind her with gasps of amazement. The young secretary drew in her breath sharply.

'Miss Benson!' she exclaimed.

In a flash Miss Lincoln took in the scene. She saw a long, oak-panelled gallery hung with numerous portraits of bewigged men and women, and containing a varied collection of all manner of antiques. A thin, middle-aged woman stood gazing horror-stricken at a beautiful vase lying shattered on the polished floor.

'The Mervyn Court vase!' breathed Dorothy, her voice strained with emotion. 'Miss Benson, please — how on earth did you get into this room?'

Miss Benson turned a vinegary, accusing eye on her questioner.

'*You* should be the one to ask questions! Young lady, I think an explanation is due from *you*. I entered here through the door, of course — and you assuring us that you locked up securely every night! Pshaw! What utter nonsense! I tell you, I was walking by a few minutes ago and I thought I'd try that door. Just on the off chance, you understand; lo and behold it was unlocked! I peeped in and saw . . . this!'

She waved a bony hand at the pitiful remnants on the floor.

Victoria stepped forward, bent to examine them.

'When was the last time you were in here, Miss Mannall?'

'Why, last evening — just after tea. I came in like I always do, for a thorough check-up. I made sure everything was all right — I tried the french window, and had a real good scout round.'

'You're absolutely sure you locked the door when you left?'

'Absolutely! I'll swear by my life I did.'

'Must have been that ghost of yours, Miss Benson!' remarked Roger Pell drily.

Miss Benson snorted her contempt. Victoria Lincoln said quietly:

'Joking aside, folks — there's something really queer going on in this house. Look at it this way: Miss Mannall saw that everything here was in order when she checked up last evening. That means that during the night someone entered here and saw fit to smash this vase.'

11

'You think it was *deliberately* smashed?' asked Roger Pell.

Victoria nodded.

'I do. For one thing, if it had fallen over there'd have been such a crash that surely someone would have heard.'

Miss Mannall cut in: 'Yes, that's sensible — because Miss Benson and Miss Gerrard have their bedrooms on either side of this gallery. You'd have heard it, I bet, Miss Benson, wouldn't you — if it had toppled over during the night?'

'Yes, young lady — I'm almost certain I would. I'm a very light sleeper. I . . . '

Victoria had bent again and was poking about on the floor amongst the shattered fragments.

'One look at this, and you'll see what I mean. See here?' The three followed her pointing finger. 'All these tiny bits never would have been made if the vase had fallen by itself. My theory is that in some way someone came in here, between — shall we say — the time Miss Mannall checked up last evening, and this morning. He or she had some good reason for smashing this vase and they made a perfect job of it. When the mysterious intruder left — well, he or she had too much to think about to remember to lock the door!'

They all straightened up as two newcomers marched in: a short, red-faced man with a very pompous manner, and a slim, pretty, fair-haired girl. Both started at the sight of the broken vase.

'Good heavens, Miss Mannall — what the devil does *this* mean?' barked the man. 'If this uncanny business isn't stopped there'll . . . '

'Oh, come!' protested Victoria, glancing reassuringly at the young secretary. 'I'm sure that Miss Mannall does her very best to protect the Professor's treasures.'

Caroline Gerrard nudged Dorothy.

'A friend in need, eh, Dot?' she whispered. 'Is this the famous sleuth you were telling us about? I'm just dying to meet her!'

'All right, Carol — I'll introduce you. Er — Miss Lincoln, this is the Professor's niece . . . Caroline Gerrard — she's from Shelburne College, and she's awfully

13

anxious to help you.'

'Well, that's very sweet of you, Carol!' Miss Lincoln smiled, shook Carol's hand warmly. 'Believe me, I'll be very *glad* of some assistance!'

'Oh, thanks, Miss Lincoln! I'll be thrilled to death, honestly . . . '

Harvey Benson broke in:

'Really, Miss Lincoln, this awful business is getting us all down. Several priceless antiques destroyed during the past week and so far we haven't the slightest clue to the culprit.'

Victoria smiled faintly.

'There's always a clue, Mr. Benson — if you know where to look for it!'

She crossed to the french windows at the far end of the gallery. First she made certain they were secure; then she noticed the small balcony outside, communicating with the bedrooms on either side of the gallery. She came back to the group. Her eyes narrowed as she looked at Miss Benson.

'Is it true that you saw a ghostly figure on this balcony last night?'

Miss Benson was emphatic.

'Absolutely! I could swear to it. I didn't go to bed till nearly midnight and I'd had a good sleep when I woke up thinking the room was stuffy. So up I rose to open the window — and that's when I saw it. She was just making for the steps at the end of the balcony, that lead down to the terrace.'

'So what did you do then?'

'Well, I — what *could* I do? Even as I looked she vanished into the shadows, walking — or rather gliding along . . . just like a ghost. I thought about following, of awakening the household — but it seemed silly, somehow. By the time we'd have gone round there, she'd have disappeared completely. Besides, it was cold and dark, and — well, I admit I was scared stiff. So I went back to bed.'

'You don't think it's possible you could have dreamt it?'

'No. The whole thing is too vivid in my memory.'

'And you're equally certain the figure was a female one?'

'I'd swear to that, too — from what I saw of it. She wore a long white robe and her hair looked dark and fluffy.'

'I see. Well, the moonlight plays queer tricks sometimes, Miss Benson. It's possible that you saw a shadow cast by the buttress of the balcony, or the wall — and the moon and your imagination did the rest. However . . . by the way, which *is* your bedroom?'

Jane Benson waved her hand vaguely.

'That one — left of the gallery. Right next door; Carol has the one on the other side.'

Victoria Lincoln spoke sternly.

'I see. Well — it's my job to see, firstly, that no more damage is done, attending to that may possibly lead to the crook. As a beginning — I'd like keys to all the doors . . . if you don't object, Miss Mannall?'

'By all means. I've one duplicate set.' The secretary handed over the bunch of keys. Victoria's shrewd dark eyes scanned the group.

'May I enquire what everyone plans to do this afternoon?'

'I'm off to the village for a few things,' Harvey Benson vouchsafed. 'And Jane is

16

coming along, too.'

Caroline said eagerly:

'I'm staying in, Miss Lincoln.'

Roger Pell said he had work on the estate to attend to, while Dorothy had her secretarial duties. One by one they filed out. Victoria took a final look at the curios, noting in particular an exquisite bronze statuette of a Greek athlete in the act of throwing a javelin. Apparently it held pride of place in the late Professor's collection, for it was placed on a magnificent ebony pedestal at the head of the gallery.

Presently the detective went out, locked the massive door securely behind her and pocketed the key.

Against the wall, a few yards away, leaned Carol Gerrard.

'Miss Lincoln — *please* . . . may I come with you? You said you'd need some help!'

Victoria slipped her arm round Carol's shoulders.

'Of course you can, my dear. I'm going for a quick look around the grounds first of all.'

'All right Miss Lincoln. I'll show you the way . . . '

They strolled out into the spacious grounds. Rain had fallen heavily on the previous night, though the brilliant sun now was rapidly drying the ground. They went round to the rear of the house, stopping on the smooth terrace beneath Miss Benson's window, with the balcony and the haunted gallery directly above them.

For a while Victoria studied the house. Then her dark eyes narrowed as she bent to examine the turf. There were footprints here — female footprints, medium size, with a distinct arrowhead marking at the heel showing that the walker had worn a certain type of rubber heel. They were plainly visible as far as the shrubbery bordering the terrace, but here they vanished completely. Miss Lincoln grinned.

'No ghost made those prints, Carol! A girl's rubber-heeled shoes . . . size about five or six. We're getting warmer!'

As they swung round to return to the house Carol noticed something that glinted in the undergrowth. Next second she'd retrieved it, her nerves tingling with excitement. It was a small hammer, its steel head muffled with a tight wrapping of cloth.

'Miss Lincoln — where d'you think this came from?'

'Ah — thanks, Carol. You've very sharp eyes, my dear. Well — it looks as if Miss Benson wasn't dreaming after all! She took the hammer, slipped it in her pocket. 'Somebody *did* get into the gallery last night — and they used this to smash that vase. Something very peculiar is going on in this house. The point is who's the culprit — and what's his or her little game?'

In the hall they met Dorothy Mannall. The young secretary caught at Victoria's sleeve.

'Any luck yet, Miss Lincoln?'

'I'm making headway, Dorothy. Don't worry about things — you're doing your best. Listen: did you have any cause to leave the house last night . . . I mean after the rain started?'

'Me? Why, no! I didn't even know it had rained till I woke up. No . . . I was in bed and fast asleep before ten — and I

19

stopped like that till eight this morning.'

'Thanks,' said Victoria. 'That's all I want to know.'

They chatted a few moments then the detective made her way upstairs, Carol following eagerly.

On the first landing they turned left, stopping outside Jane Benson's room. Softly Victoria turned the knob, pushed the door open.

'Carol!' she whispered. 'Stay here and keep watch. If anyone comes, give a little whistle.'

Carol fairly trembled with excitement.

'All right, Miss Lincoln! I'll watch out for you . . .'

Leaving the door ajar Victoria entered the room. Against a rail at the bottom of a built-in wardrobe leaned three pairs of shoes. Swiftly she bent to examine them; a whistle of disappointment presently escaped her lips. Neither of the pairs were soiled, and neither was the size she sought. She went out, beckoned to Carol. On the opposite side to the gallery door, and further up, was Dorothy Mannall's room. Quietly they went over. Again

20

Victoria tried the door. It, too, was open. Nodding quickly over her shoulder to Carol, she pushed it open, entered.

The young secretary's tidiness was apparent. The few articles of clothing left out were nearly folded and placed on a chair; and from beneath it peeped the mud-caked rubber heels of a pair of shoes!

Miss Lincoln caught in her breath sharply as she bent, gently pulled them out. They were still damp from contact with wet earth. She turned them over. The new rubber heels bore plainly the unmistakable arrowhead design. And under the instep was stamped the size . . . 5!

Frowning, the detective shoved them back beneath the chair. One question burned in her brain: was the pleasant young woman who'd called her in to solve this baffling mystery herself the secret enemy?

★   ★   ★

Victoria Lincoln's brows were creased in thought as she went out, and quietly closed the door.

Carol said breathlessly:

'Did you find anything, Miss Lincoln?'

'Yes. Now listen, Carol: if I tell you something — can I trust you to keep it absolutely to yourself?'

'Yes, Miss Lincoln! Honestly you can . . . '

Speaking softly, Victoria revealed what she'd discovered in the secretary's room.

'Dot Mannall!' Carol gasped. 'Why, it doesn't seem possible! She's so quiet, and — well, so *decent* . . . '

'I agree. It's quite obvious, too, that she was devoted to the Professor. I don't like to think she's the unknown enemy. Yet the idea of a ghost smashing valuable ornaments for no good reason . . . why, it's too ridiculous for words!'

They walked slowly downstairs, through the hall, out into the garden. Already the light was fading. In another hour it would be dusk.

'Let's have another look round the back,' Victoria said.

Presently they were mounting the steps leading to the balcony; and next moment they stood outside the french windows of the haunted gallery.

They were firmly locked still. Carol kept close to the detective as they gazed in through the thick glass. Inside the gallery the light was hazy, but they could just distinguish the framed portraits and the antiques displayed on tables and pedestals. Victoria's glance wandered to the door. Next second her mouth gaped wide with amazement.

For the gallery door stood ajar, though she'd locked it herself less than two hours ago — the key was in her pocket now. Dorothy Mannall held the only other key!

Victoria stared in utter bewilderment; and as she did so, for an instant of time she caught sight of a figure vanishing through the door. It moved too swiftly in that uncertain light for her to be sure whether it was male or female. She saw only the blur of a long white garment as the ghostly intruder disappeared.

Miss Lincoln gripped Carol's arm:

'Look — did you see that?'

'Yes . . . a figure in white! What on earth can it be?'

'We'll find out, Carol. Come on! Let's

see how you can run!'

They raced down the steps and round to the front. In less than ten seconds they were pelting through the hall; and as they did so a woman's terrified scream rang through the house!

Victoria bounded up the stairs, Carol on her heels. At the top she paused, every nerve in her body tensed. A woman lay motionless on the landing near the gallery door, her face deathly white, her arms flung out. Victoria stepped up quickly.

'Jane Benson!' she gasped dropping to her knees at her side.

Miss Benson was unconscious, in a dead faint. Carol sped to the bathroom, returning with a tumbler of water. Victoria held the glass to Miss Benson's lips, forcing the liquid into her mouth. As she did so Harvey Benson came hurrying up the stairs. 'I was in the kitchen,' he said. 'I heard the — someone screamed . . . oh, dear . . . it's poor Jane . . . '

In a moment Jane moaned slightly, opened her eyes. Then down the stairs, from the landing above, came Roger Pell, looking very flustered and agitated. He peered down at Miss Benson, then at Victoria.

'Good heavens! What on earth has happened now, ma'am? This poor girl — she . . . ?'

Jane Benson sat up with a wan smile.

'Sorry I caused such a fuss, folks. As I crossed the landing something — well, sprang out at me . . . I couldn't see what or who. I was so dead scared I must have fainted right away. Terribly silly of me . . . '

'I can understand how you felt, Miss Benson,' Victoria said. 'Just before you screamed Carol and I were outside, on the balcony. I swear I saw someone pass through the gallery door. We raced round — we were in the hall when you screamed. I . . . '

Roger Pell cut in: 'You say you saw someone pass through the gallery door? Why — didn't you lock it when you left? I saw Dot give you the keys! Don't say you . . . '

'Why, I saw you lock it, Miss Lincoln,' Carol broke in. 'I was standing here when . . . '

'Oh, I locked it all right,' Victoria said grimly. 'But let's take a look at it now.'

She sped over, the others hard on her heels. When she tried the knob the door opened immediately! No one spoke as they all crowded in. At first glance everything seemed to be in order. Victoria commenced a quick check-up of the collection as more footsteps sounded outside.

Dorothy Mannall came in.

'What's happened now?' she wanted to know. 'I felt a bit head-achy after lunch so I went to my study for a nap. Then I heard the commotion and . . .'

Her voice broke off. With a startled cry she pointed towards it. 'It's gone!' cried Dorothy. 'The bronze statuette! It's missing . . .'

Miss Lincoln's hand on her arm was reassuring.

'Take it easy, Dorothy — and don't worry about the statuette. I think I can promise you that our unknown enemy has struck for the last time!'

★   ★   ★

After tea Victoria learned that Professor Marchant's solicitor — a Mr. Hilary Mitchell — was due at midnight for the reading of the will. They were all seated at the table, wondering what to do with the rest of the evening.

'It's rather a peculiar time for the job, isn't it? Midnight?' Victoria said.

Miss Benson's voice was prim.

'The dear Professor was like that, Miss Lincoln. Always very eccentric.' She jumped up. 'Well, I'm off to bed for a few hours. I need sleep.'

Harvey Benson said he'd doze by the fire in the lounge. Roger Pell had some clerical work to do in his study; and Dorothy Mannall pleading a rotten headache, said she too was going to bed till about eleven o'clock.

As for Victoria Lincoln — she had her own plans. She intended to keep watch in the haunted gallery!

Carol lingered after the others had walked out.

'Carol, I'm going to do some spook-watching,' Victoria said. 'Like to come along?'

'You mean — you're going to sit in the haunted gallery . . . keeping watch?'

'Right first time! Are you game?'

'You bet I am, Miss Lincoln!'

So shortly after eight they entered the room of mystery. They pulled up chairs to the long windows, sat staring out across the moonlit grounds. Time passed slowly, but Victoria had plenty of problems to keep her brain occupied.

After a while she turned to Carol.

'I'm going to ask you to be very brave, my dear. I want you to stay here alone for about ten minutes — I have another little job I must do.'

In the gloom Carol's hands clenched tightly on the arms of her chair.

'Y-es, Miss Lincoln. I'll stay. Come back quickly, though, won't you?'

Victoria smiled, patted Carol's shoulder.

'You've plenty of grit, kid,' she murmured.

She went softly out and down the landing. She found Dorothy Mannall's door unlocked. The young secretary was sleeping peacefully but Victoria awakened her gently. She sat on the bed for half an hour, talked earnestly with Dorothy. Then she repeated her admonition not to worry, and went back to the gallery.

From the gloom Carol whispered:

'All clear, Miss Lincoln! No move from the ghostie yet!'

Eleven strokes boomed from the church tower clock. Quarter-past . . . half-past. Victoria began to wonder if their vigil would be in vain. Then she sat bolt upright as stealthy footsteps sounded from the far end of the gallery near the door!

Softly she rose to her feet as the mysterious intruder flashed a torch. Foot by foot she edged towards the newcomer who was selecting another curio to destroy, for it seemed he put his torch beam first on one and then on another. Straining her eyes through the gloom Victoria saw a sudden dark blur of movement as the intruder raised his arm.

Next second came a splintering crash as a heavy object fell in fragments to the floor. Flashing her torch Victoria leapt forward. But the intruder moved with lightning speed. In her torch beam Victoria saw nothing but the end of a thick walking stick disappearing through the door!

They were outside and on the landing in a matter of seconds, but the corridor was deserted! Then the bedroom door on the left of the gallery opened and out came Jane Benson.

'Something else battered to pieces?' she asked coldly. 'I heard the crash. What's happened?'

Before Victoria could answer her, Harvey Benson and Roger Pell came running down from the landing above them. The detective beckoned them into the gallery, switched on the lights. The massive ebony pedestal that had held the bronze statuette was lying on the floor smashed to smithereens!

They all bent to look. From her handbag Victoria took a small packet, sprinkled some white powder on the black shiny pieces of ebony. After a moment she seized one, examined it, then slipped it in her bag.

'A clue?' asked Jane Benson. Harvey Benson and Roger Pell stepped back a pace.

Miss Lincoln answered gravely:

'Maybe. I said before — there's always a clue if you know where to look! Remember?' She glanced at her watch. 'Ten to twelve, folks. I think Mr. Mitchell will be waiting for us in the lounge. Shall we go down?'

Outside on the landing they had another shock. Victoria Lincoln raised a warning hand.

'Look!' Her voice was tense. 'Not a sound, anyone!'

Everyone stared. Gliding silently towards them along the broad landing was the figure of a young woman, wearing a long white dressing gown over her pyjamas. Her eyes were open but it was obvious she did not see the amazed group of watchers, In her arms she carried the missing bronze statuette!

It was Dorothy Mannall!

'You see?' Victoria spoke softly. 'Miss Mannall is a sleepwalker. Subconsciously she's been trying to protect the gift promised her by her late employer. I'll take her back to her room — she must be awakened very carefully. Will the rest go down to the lounge, please? We'll join you in a few moments.'

Half an hour later the will had been read and Hilary Mitchell was on his way back to London. Jane and Harvey Benson and Caroline each had been left a substantial sum of money; while Dorothy, as a token of her faithful service, received the bronze statuette as promised by the Professor.

After Mitchell had gone, coffee and biscuits were served. Dorothy was awake now and properly dressed, though very quiet and subdued at the disclosure of her sleepwalking. She sat in the background looking ill at ease.

Roger Pell put down his cup and said impatiently:

'Well, folks — what now? Are we safe to go to bed?' He turned to Victoria. 'Are we any nearer solving the mystery of the shattered antiques, Miss Lincoln?'

Victoria Lincoln rose. Now was the time for her to spring her trap! Her voice was steady.

'Yes — we're getting on gradually, Mr. Pell. I've reasoned things out like this: somebody is smashing those antiques because he — or she — is looking for something. See the idea? Hidden away in one of those curios is a valuable treasure — a jewel, an heirloom — something like that. This person somehow discovered that; obviously it's someone who was fairly close to the Professor and in his confidence.

'Now the shock of her employer's death brought on Miss Mannall's odd, childish habit of sleepwalking. Our mysterious friend seized on this to gain access to the gallery. For most nights, I expect, Dorothy — while sleepwalking — went to the gallery to look over the antiques, to make sure they were safe . . . and most times she forgot to relock the door. This person saw her one night and thereafter kept watch, each time following into the gallery after Dorothy had left.

'The night before I came he followed Dorothy into the grounds, noticing the peculiar footprints, no doubt. He planted a small hammer for me to find, to put me off the scent — to lead me to suppose that the owner of those footprints was also the one who was doing all the damage.

'To come to this afternoon: Dorothy decided to take a nap, but her anxiety for the statuette prevailed and she came, in her sleep, to collect it. Carol and I actually saw her going out through the door. We were on the balcony, having a look round. Dorothy it would be too, who gave Miss Benson such a scare!'

Harvey Benson wanted to know if everything was all right now.

'Is this dashed bloke, or whoever it is — I mean, what about this treasure you're talking about? Will he — ?'

Victoria beckoned to Dorothy, who was silently holding the statuette.

'Bring that over here, Miss Mannell, please. We may find the answer to Mr. Benson's question.'

Dorothy obeyed. Victoria carefully examined the exquisite figure. Then suddenly, with a deft movement of her fingers, she twisted its head. With a faint click the base of the statuette swung open, revealing a cavity — and something there that flashed with a thousand fires!

The detective shook it into her palm. A long, lustrous diamond necklace . . . a magnificent piece of priceless jewellery.

Gasps of amazement and admiration went up on all sides.

'Here's the answer, Mr. Benson!' Victoria Lincoln said. 'There'll be no more trouble over the curios getting destroyed. I think, also, that I've the answer to our last and greatest problem: who is this mysterious person who was smashing them in his search for this necklace?'

The babbling tongues grew silent,

'Really?' said Jane Benson eagerly. 'Goodness, you *have* been clever, Miss Lincoln! Whoever is it?'

Victoria took out her wallet, extracted the piece of ebony she'd taken from the floor of the gallery, and which still held remnants of the white powder.

'After tea this evening,' she said, looking sternly at the expectant gathering, 'Carol and I went to keep watch in the haunted gallery. We left the door unlocked on purpose. About eleven-thirty our mysterious enemy, on the prowl as usual, found it open and crept in, this time selecting the ebony pedestal. He smashed it with a walking stick, after feeling all round it in case there was a hidden catch or spring.'

Victoria Lincoln paused dramatically.

'Here it was he made his big mistake! He left a perfect set of fingerprints on this piece.' She held up this jagged segment. 'I spotted them immediately I dusted the fragments with that powder. So all we have to do now is, take a sample of everyone's fingerprints — and we'll soon have the guilty party!'

There was a sudden scuffle as Roger Pell sprang for the door.

Victoria said sharply:

'There he is — don't let him get away!'

Harvey Benson dived at Pell's legs, brought him crashing to the ground. Carol snatched up a cushion, banged it on Pell's head, then sat on it triumphantly! She screamed:

'Quick, Miss Lincoln — tie his hands . . . he's getting up . . .'

Victoria had her bag open. Next second a pair of handcuffs gleamed on the estate manager's wrists, and before he could gather his scattered wits Carol had grabbed a silken cover from the settee and thrust it at Harvey Benson.

'Tie his legs, Mr. Benson!' she gasped. 'Quickly . . . '

Harvey Benson wasted no time. Next moment Roger Pell was a helpless prisoner, tied hand and foot.

Miss Lincoln calmly picked up the 'phone, asked for the police station.

'All bluff, of course!' Victoria Lincoln explained to an admiring group. 'There weren't any fingerprints on that bit of ebony at all, but it trapped the culprit — and solved the mystery of the haunted gallery!'

Before she left, Victoria had a little talk with Caroline.

'Look, my dear — how much longer have you to do at Shelburne?'

'I'm on my last term now, Miss Lincoln. Why?'

'Well . . . we seem to get along swimmingly together, don't we? And the point is: I need an assistant. You're a smart intelligent girl, Caroline. What d'you think of the idea?'

For a moment Carol couldn't speak.

Presently she gasped:

'Oh, Miss Lincoln . . . I'd love to come and work for you!'

'Well, I'll write to your folks, Carol. By the way, that's rather important . . . my offices are in Regent Street. Is your home in London?'

'Yes, Miss Lincoln . . . we live in Kensington — in Cheyne Walk.'

'Couldn't be better, my dear! A short bus ride brings you right to my door.'

'You mean it, Miss Lincoln? You'll honestly write to my parents and ask them?'

'I promise, Carol. Shall we shake on it?'

The world seemed an enchanted place to Caroline as Victoria Lincoln smilingly extended her hand.

2

The Clue of the Blue Powder

Dusk was falling as Victoria Lincoln stopped her car on the wide roundabout fronting the little station of Denbury. She'd called to collect a parcel of books she was expecting from London, on the five-twenty train.

She went to the office, signed the necessary forms, gathered up her parcel; as she came out of the station she noticed a pretty, dark-haired girl standing forlornly under the portico.

When she saw Victoria she came over quickly.

'I hope you'll excuse me, ma'am — but d'you know where I could hire a taxi, or perhaps a pony and trap?'

Miss Lincoln smiled.

'What — in Denbury? My dear young lady, you're asking the impossible! May I ask where you are bound for?'

'I want to get to Riverdale Hall . . . it's

a big country house about four miles away.'

'Oh — yes, I know the place. Well, hop in my car, my dear. I'm going quite near there myself.'

'Are you really? That's, awfully kind of you! I've left my luggage on the platform. I'll slip and get it.'

'I'll give you a hand.'

The girl's two suitcases were a little way down the platform, outside the ladies' waiting room. As they bent to pick them up Victoria caught the girl's arm.

'Have you seen this?' she asked, pointing to the words chalked across the larger one. 'It looks rather peculiar!'

The girl's delicate face paled.

'Good heavens!' she gasped. 'D'you know, that's the third message I've had like that!' Slowly she read the words:

IF YOU VALUE YOUR LIFE,
KEEP AWAY FROM THE
GREEN ROOM!

Miss Lincoln frowned. 'You're sure it wasn't on when you put these cases down?'

'I'm certain. I'm sure to have noticed it

40

when I pulled them off the rack.'

'I suppose so. Then the practical joker must be hanging round the station now. Who d'you suppose it is?'

'Well . . . somehow I don't think it *is* a joke. I think the — '

She broke off as old Tom Dobson, the porter, came from his office. Victoria Lincoln called him over.

'Tom — have you seen anyone hanging round near these cases?'

Tom scratched his head.

'No, ma'am — that I haven't. I been busy in my office, a-checking them consignment notes. Why — is anything wrong, Miss Lincoln?'

'No — it's all right, Tom.'

She turned to the girl.

'I suggest we get moving, young lady. I don't think we'll discover very much around here.'

They went out to the car, stowed the bags in the luggage boot. As they rolled down the station drive the girl turned excitedly to Victoria Lincoln. 'I say — did I hear that porter call you Miss Lincoln?'

'You did; and how'd you like to

introduce *yourself*?'

'I'd love to — I mean ... I'm Anne Seymour — I'm at Shelburne College, in the Fifth ... the reason I asked about your name is that our head girl is always talking about you. You know her, don't you ... Caroline Gerrard?'

'Oh, surely — very good-looking child ... blonde, blue eyed ... yes, Carol and I have had quite a few exploits together. Matter of fact, she's coming to help me when she leaves Shelburne at the end of this term.'

'Yes, I know.' Anne smiled. 'Believe me, the whole school knows too! Carol simply can't talk of anything else. We all think she's the luckiest thing on earth, Miss Lincoln!'

'Time will tell!' Victoria murmured.

They turned into the main street.

'Is your home down this way, Miss Lincoln?' Anne asked.

'Well, I have a cottage not far from Riverdale Hall. I slip down here for weekends as often as I can. Now — suppose you tell me a little more about yourself? I'm very interested in these

42

threatening messages!'

'Well, Miss Lincoln — I was born at Riverdale, and lived there till about three years ago. Then my father secured an important post near London so we moved into a smaller house nearer town. Recently he had a very good offer for the place from some people who want to turn it into a kind of small country hotel for elderly folk — so he's selling it. Our Christmas holidays started a few days ago, so I've come down to the old place for a few days, just to say goodbye, kind of thing. I know it sounds awfully silly and sentimental. Dad laughed at me when I suggested it but my mother said it was a good idea.'

'I think I'd do the same thing in your place, Anne. Is anyone there to look after you?'

'Oh, yes. Mr. and Mrs. Hunter — they were our domestics when we lived there, and Dad let them stay on to keep the place in order. There's Barlow also, the gardener.'

'I see. And what will they do when the place is sold?'

'Oh, Dad says he's taken care of that. He says he'll make an agreement with whoever buys Riverdale, that they'll be allowed to keep their jobs.'

Victoria nodded slowly.

'Isn't is rather strange that there was no one at the station to meet you? I mean, they must have known you were coming, surely?'

'Yes — I wrote and told Mrs. Hunter the day and the time. I fully expected Hunter to be there with the trap. Something must have happened to have kept him at the Hall.'

'It must have. Now — you say you've had two other mysterious messages besides the one scribbled on your suitcase?'

'Yes . . . two unsigned notes, posted to my home address, with very much the same words — that I'd be in terrible danger if I went near the Green Room!'

Victoria said slowly:

'Then it seems that whoever wrote them has something to do with the Hall, and also knows your address. Can you make any guesses, Anne?'

'Well, there's only Mr. and Mrs.

Hunter. It's simply ridiculous to suppose it's them. Why, they've been with us ever since I can remember!'

'H'm'm . . . it's certainly an extraordinary business. What is this Green Room, by the way?'

'Why, it's my old nursery, Miss Lincoln. I say — could you possibly come to Riverdale with me . . . I mean, stay for supper, perhaps spend the night with us?'

'Yes — I rather think I'd like to, Anne. I've an idea there's more behind those messages than meets the eye.'

'Oh, thanks, Miss Lincoln. I'd be really grateful if you could find out something about them.'

For the next quarter of an hour they rode in silence, as the shadows deepened over the silent countryside.

Then Victoria turned in at the gates of a rambling old stone house, standing back from the road in well-kept grounds. The detective noted the flush that crept into Anne's cheeks as she saw her childhood home.

'It hasn't changed one scrap, Miss Lincoln!' she breathed. 'I've had some marvellous times here . . . '

As they rounded the drive the front door opened. Out came a kindly-faced, elderly woman in a black silky dress, and a tall dignified, snowy-haired man.

Anne jumped down, ran forward.

'Nan!' she cried. 'I'm so glad to see you again!'

They held each other in a long embrace, then Anne shook hands with Mr. Hunter and introduced Victoria Lincoln.

'Nan, didn't you get my letter about the train?' asked Anne presently. 'I was surprised when no one met me at the station. I'd have been in a fine pickle but for Miss Lincoln!'

The old housekeeper looked puzzled.

'Letter, Miss Anne? The only one we've had from you was one a week ago saying you were thinking of coming for a few days soon. We've had nothing since.'

Anne and Victoria exchanged significant glances.

'Probably the letter's been delayed,' suggested Miss Lincoln. She told the Hunters about the threatening messages. The startled expression that flashed suddenly into Mrs. Hunter's eyes was not lost on the detective.

'Why — it's extraordinary!' muttered Mr. Hunter. 'Why should anyone imagine harm coming to Anne in her old home?'

Victoria, however, had seen the quick glance that had passed between the aged couple.

'Tell me, Mrs. Hunter — who knew Anne was coming — besides yourselves?'

'Eh? Why . . . we mentioned it to quite a few . . . Ted Barlow, the gardener, for one — Mr. Drayke, the vicar, Percy Higgins, the milkman . . . aye, and Mr. Cranmer, him from London who's taking an inventory of the place . . . and Tom Jensen, the postman . . . '

'I see. This Mr. Cranmer . . . is he staying here — I mean, is he sleeping here?'

'Aye, that he is. He will be too, so he says, till after the sale next week.'

They were standing in the hall now. Anne said eagerly;

'Nan, I'm dying to see my old nursery! In spite of those stupid letters — I'm still going to sleep in there. They won't scare me. No fear!'

There was a sudden clatter as the housekeeper dropped the large bunch of keys she was carrying. Her husband stooped quickly to retrieve them. Then in a low voice he said:

'Miss Anne, I shouldn't if I were you. We've heard such queer noises coming from there lately — we're beginning to think it's haunted! Aren't we, Ma?'

'Aye, that we are!' agreed Mrs. Hunter. 'Knockings and shufflings and such-like. Three times we've rushed in to see, but there's never been anyone there.' She shook her head sagely. 'You be a wise child, Miss Anne, and keep away from it.'

Victoria Lincoln saw the colour fade from Anne's face. Nevertheless the schoolgirl laughed gaily, took the keys from Mrs. Hunter.

'Rubbish, Nan! No ghostie will keep me out of my old nursery. Shall we go up now, Miss Lincoln?'

On the first landing Anne paused before a door painted a pale green.

'Here we are, Miss Lincoln! The famous Green Room, where I've spent some of my happiest hours!'

She threw the door open. Victoria followed her in quickly. And next moment a cry of horror broke from Anne's lips.

The whole room was in a chaotic state. Chairs were overturned, cushions and pillows flung here and there, a mirror above the mantelpiece had been swept to the floor, where it lay shattered; and across the space where it had hung had been scrawled the words:

'BE WARNED IN TIME!
KEEP AWAY FROM THIS ROOM
WHILE YOU ARE YET SAFE!'

Anne squatted on the bed, her pretty, oval face set grimly.

'Miss Lincoln — what does all this mean? Who can have done this to my room?'

Victoria's dark eyes flashed.

'Your secret enemy is a very determined one, Anne! At all costs he or she intends to keep you out of here.'

Both turned as footsteps sounded on the landing. Mr. and Mrs. Hunter stood fearfully in the doorway, surveying the damage.

The old lady clutched her husband's

49

arm, pointed a trembling finger at the writing on the wall.

'Miss Anne, don't stay in here! Come away before some dreadful harm befalls you!'

Anne said:

'All right, Nan — we'll see.'

The old couple went out. Victoria walked to the window, bent to examine something on the polished floor.

Presently she called Anne over.

'See this, my dear? A footprint — with traces of a yellowish clay, I'm pretty sure it's come from that stretch of soft ground near the station entrance. Things are beginning to add up, Anne!'

'It looks like it. You mean the same person who put that warning on my suitcase has been at work here?'

'Exactly,' Miss Lincoln pointed to an oblong patch on the wall near the door. 'Look, Anne — a picture has hung there — and recently. D'you remember it?'

'Why, yes — 'Alice Blue Gown', I used to call it. A picture of a beautiful lady in a blue crinoline. Who's taken it away, I wonder?'

'We'll find out. Let's go and see Mother Hunter.'

The housekeeper looked a little worried when they asked her.

'Oh, Mr. Cranmer took it down. He insisted on having all the pictures locked in one room till he had time to value them.'

'Where is it now?' Anne asked. 'I'd love to see it again.'

'All right, my dear — so you shall. I'll get him to show you them all, after supper. Miss Anne — you're not thinking of sleeping in the Green Room tonight?'

Anne caught Miss Lincoln's eye. The detective inclined her head slightly. Anne said:

'I really think I shall, Nan. We'll never solve this mystery by being frightened of it, will we?'

Victoria gave Anne's arm a reassuring squeeze as they walked in to supper.

* * *

After supper Victoria Lincoln went to her room and spent a quiet half hour considering the baffling mystery of the Green Room. Then she slipped out and went softly along the landing.

In this part of the house there were three other rooms besides the Green Room. Two of them Victoria found to be little but lumber rooms. But the third, next to the Green Room, was securely locked. From her bag the detective took a ring on which were four slim skeleton keys. At the third attempt the lock clicked back. Looking quickly up and down the landing, she pushed open the door, slipped inside.

She was satisfied with what she saw. Here was the room where Cranmer had stored the Riverdale collection of pictures, for it was stacked almost from floor to ceiling; and a few minutes' search amongst them gave confirmation of Mrs. Hunter's statement. 'Alice Blue Gown' was there all right! Victoria found it on top of a pile of miniatures; a lovely piece of work in the best Rembrandt style.

Miss Lincoln gazed disappointedly round the room. There seemed nothing here that would help solve the mystery of the threatening messages. She'd turned to leave when her keen eyes noticed something in a corner near the door.

Swiftly she bent to examine it, touching it softly with her dainty forefinger. It was a thin film of powder; fine, and pale blue in colour. Victoria straightened, went softly out. She was deep in thought as she walked along the landing towards the Green Room.

Light came from under the door. She knocked. Anne opened it immediately.

'Anne — I've the beginnings of an idea!' Victoria said. 'D'you mind if I have a look round your room?'

'Of course not. Come in, Miss Lincoln.'

The detective went straight to a tall cupboard in a corner on the right of the window. She gave a murmur of satisfaction as she saw a few grains of bluish powder on the floor nearby . . . the same powder that had been dropped in the picture room next door!

Anne watched interestedly as Victoria pulled open the cupboard door. Inside was a litter of toys, a badly battered doll, picture books and other childish treasures.

Miss Lincoln's attention was fastened on the back of the cupboard. She played her torch beam over it and as she turned round a soft whistle escaped her lips.

'More food for thought, Anne!' she murmured. 'Let's go down and join the others, shall we?'

'Food for thought, Miss Lincoln? You mean you've found a clue in the cupboard?' Anne's voice was eager, excited.

'It's given me a lead towards a solution, my dear. All we can do now is await developments.'

Standing before the fire in the lounge was Mr. Cranmer, the auctioneer — a dark, slim gentleman in an immaculate suit. He hadn't been in to supper. Mrs. Hunter introduced Victoria. As they shook hands the young detective strove to read what lay behind Cranmer's cold eyes.

'I've been in Denbury all afternoon on business, Miss Lincoln,' he said quietly. 'And what do you think of Riverdale?'

'A delightful old place, indeed,' Miss Lincoln said primly. Idly she glanced down at Cranmer's neat, pointed shoes. Her dark eyes gleamed as she noticed there several distinct splashes of yellowish clay!

'Am I right in surmising your business took you near the station, Mr. Cranmer?' Victoria asked.

He shot her a quick glance.

'Why — er . . . yes . . . I went to the bookstall for a magazine I was unable to get in town.' He paused. 'Why? Did you see me there?'

At that moment someone knocked on the door. Mrs. Hunter opened it. Victoria saw a short, burly figure in black jacket and trousers, holding a tray on which were a coffee pot and cups.

'Ah, come in, Barlow,' said Mrs. Hunter. 'You'll take coffee, Miss Lincoln? And you, Mr. Cranmer? I know Miss Anne will!'

Barlow went to the sideboard, poured out the coffee. Anne nudged Victoria.

'The gardener,' she whispered. 'Mrs. Hunter's making sure he earns his money by making him a part-time butler!'

When they had their coffee Victoria drew Anne aside. She spoke softly.

'Listen, Anne: let them think you're sleeping in the Green Room tonight. We'll go up to bed shortly and about eleven I'll come to your room and you sleep in mine. See the idea? We'll change over. I honestly think there's danger for you there.'

'You do? All right, Miss Lincoln — I'll do whatever you say.'

They lingered awhile chatting to Mr. Cranmer. Then Anne played a few of her old pieces on the piano and Miss Lincoln, who was a keen musician, listened in appreciative silence.

Before they went upstairs Anne remembered 'Alice Blue Gown'.

'Oh, Mrs. Hunter — give me the key to the picture room, there's a dear. I must have a look at dear old Alice!'

Mrs. Hunter fumbled in her pocket, rose.

'All right, Miss Anne. I'll take you up now if you like.'

In the room it didn't take Anne many moments to spot the picture. Then from the door Miss Lincoln heard her exclamation of amazement. She went forward. Anne was holding the portrait at arm's length, her pretty face creased with puzzled annoyance.

'Anything wrong, Anne?' asked Victoria Lincoln.

'There certainly is! This isn't my 'Alice Blue Gown'. It's something like it, I admit — but it's not the one I left behind!'

Mrs. Hunter looked over her shoulder.

'You're certain. Miss Anne? It looks just the same to me!'

Victoria peered closely. What Anne said was true. This wasn't the same picture she'd seen barely two hours ago when she'd let herself in with the skeleton key . . .

They trooped out in silence. Mrs. Hunter locked up, went downstairs. Miss Lincoln accompanied Anne down the landing to the Green Room. Anne sat on the bed swinging her legs impatiently.

'I wonder what the dickens is going on in this house?' she demanded. 'Why on earth should anyone want to mess about with Alice? That picture's been changed. Miss Lincoln! I'll swear to it!'

'I won't argue about it, my dear. We'll tackle Cranmer in the morning — see what he has to say. Meanwhile, I suggest you leave the Green Room to me. You slip to my room and get a nice long sleep.'

They chatted a few moments then said goodnight. When she was alone Miss Lincoln set to work quickly. From a reel in her handbag she took a length of black cotton, fastened one end to the handle of the big cupboard. The other end she tied to an old-fashioned hand-bell she'd spotted, fixed on the wall behind the bed.

Then she switched off the light and lay down, prepared for a long vigil.

Sleep seemed very near. Vaguely she wandered what had made her so tired, No matter . . . if any intruder came exploring, the cotton would set the bell ringing . . .

Gradually her head sank back on the pillows; her eyes closed, her breathing became deep and even.

Midnight tolled from a nearby church tower. A heavy silence shut down over the sleeping countryside.

Another half-hour ticked by. Then, slowly, stealthily; the handle of the door began to turn.

Victoria Lincoln opened her eyes, lay staring dully into the darkness. Carefully she passed a hand over her throbbing brow. What had happened? Had she — in spite of her determination — fallen asleep?

She rolled off the bed, stood up with difficulty. Her legs felt leaden, her whole body ached with weariness. Switching on the light, she noted the time: a quarter to three. No doubt about it at all . . . she had fallen asleep.

A glance at the cupboard caused her to start forward. The cotton was broken! Victoria became conscious then of an unnatural lethargy; more — she felt she'd been struggling to awaken from it for some time past. The broken cotton supplied the missing link to the puzzle.

'That's it!' Victoria muttered. 'Somehow, our mysterious enemy has given me a sleeping draught — to make sure I'd be powerless when he or she came prowling!'

Here her hands clenched suddenly, for she remembered that no one had known she was sleeping in the Green Room that night. No one, that is, save the girl she was trying to help — Anne Seymour!

Had the drug been intended for Anne? Or . . . was Anne the secret enemy after all?

Her brows drawn in thought, the detective went over to the cupboard, pulled open the door, groped over the woodwork at the back. Presently there was a faint click, and a gaping cavity appeared in the wall.

Miss Lincoln flashed her torch, her heart beating fast with excitement. The beam revealed the room next door that was being used as a picture gallery. Stepping softly, Victoria went through. Next moment she crouched back in the shadows as a key was inserted in the lock. Slowly the door creaked open . . .

Palely gleaming, a shaft of moonlight slanted through the un-curtained window and across the door. Scarcely daring to breathe, Victoria watched. Stealthily, a slim, girlish figure crept in. Miss Lincoln could barely repress a low whistle of amazement.

Anne Seymour!

The detective's face was grim as she saw Anne make towards the pile on which lay the portrait of 'Alice Blue Gown'. Next second the black shadows of the far wall had swallowed her.

Silence. Victoria decided to count twenty, then spring out and surprise Anne. What on earth was the schoolgirl's game, she wondered. She'd reached eleven when a soft rustling came from her right. She turned, then caught in her breath sharply. She saw a pair of malevolent eyes watching her from the darkness — eyes that peered, glinting, through the slits of a mask!

Miss Lincoln's scream died on her lips as the masked intruder leapt. Next second a rough muffler, whipped round her mouth, effectively stifled her cries. Taken completely off balance, she was dumped in a chair and securely tied.

She had to struggle for breath through the scarf's choking folds. Dazedly, she saw her captor go to a pile of pictures and begin to sort them over, putting some in one pile, some in another — working by the light of a small torch. Through the gloom Miss Lincoln strained her eyes till they felt like bursting. Who was that shadowy, masked figure? Could it be — Anne Seymour . . . ?

Five minutes passed. Then the door

burst open again and a deep voice said:

'All right, you scoundrel — put up your hands! The game's up . . . '

From the doorway, moonlight glinted on the revolver in the newcomer's hand. With a coarse oath the masked intruder turned from his task and leapt for the door. There was a desperate scuffle as the two closed. Across the room they rolled in a fierce struggle. Miss Lincoln saw the revolver butt raised . . . twice it crashed down on the masked one's head. For a moment, legs thrashed wildly . . . then there was silence, and a prone figure stretched out on the floor . . .

Slowly the victor stood up, went to the door, switched on the light. Miss Lincoln gave a stifled gasp of amazement as she saw the dishevelled figure of Mr. Cranmer, the auctioneer — and just behind him, leaning in a corner, the white, startled face of Anne Semour!

Cranmer cut Victoria's bounds. She stood up, rubbing her sore wrists. She nodded her thanks to the auctioneer, then smiled at Anne.

'Now we'll see who the real crook is,

my dear,' she said. 'The one who's robbed you of Alice, and many other pictures worth thousands of pounds. I've a good idea who it is, too!'

Anne and Mr. Cranmer watched as she bent, snatched off the mask of the unconscious man. Gasps of amazement went up as there lay revealed the features of Ted Barlow, the gardener!

'Just as I thought!' went on the detective. 'I suspected Barlow when I found traces of a special fertilising powder in here and in the Green Room. Only a gardener would use such a powder, and traces of it naturally would cling to his clothes.'

'What was his game, though, Miss Lincoln?' Anne asked dazedly.

'Just this — Barlow was determined to steal the most valuable of these pictures — substituting them with fakes before Mr. Cranmer had valued them. When they were all locked in this room, however, he knew the only way he could get in was through the secret panel in your old toy cupboard in the Green Room. When Mrs. Hunter told him you were coming to stay here till after the sale, he became very worried . . . knowing you'd be sleeping in your old nursery, and would hear him on his thieving expeditions. So he intercepted your letters, and did his best to prevent you coming; witness the messages he sent you through the post and his last-minute attempt at the station.

'Then tonight, he put a drug in your coffee to keep you asleep while he changed the rest of the pictures. Thinking I might be troublesome, he drugged mine, too — to be on the safe side!'

She turned to the auctioneer.

'Now, Mr. Cranmer — I suggest you 'phone the police and get Barlow here locked up. I fancy we'll find quite a collection of valuable paintings in his lodge!'

The auctioneer shook Victoria's hand warmly.

'A very smart piece of work, Miss Lincoln! I'm very glad indeed that I was able to help!'

He went out to 'phone, first securing the gardener's arms and legs with the rope that had bound Miss Lincoln.

Victoria slipped her arm round Anne's shoulders.

'Let's slip down and make some tea, shall we? And how about telling me what you were doing in here tonight?'

Anne grinned.

'Well, I woke up about half-past two with my head aching like billy-o, Miss Lincoln. I bet yours was, too, after that awful sleeping stuff! I kept thinking about 'Alice', and the dreadful way she'd changed. I just had to get up and come and look at her again, to make sure I hadn't been seeing things. I was hardly through the door before I heard sounds of a struggle — then I caught sight of the masked man!'

Her eyes were wide with excitement. 'Oh, Miss Lincoln — I was scared stiff! I raced out, into the Green Room — but you weren't there. So I woke up Mr. Cranmer and he came back with me — and we nabbed the thief red-handed!'

Victoria Lincoln smiled.

'It's been a very entertaining interlude, Anne. To think I came down to Denbury for a quiet weekend!'

3

The Thief of Claygate Farm

Victoria Lincoln sat at her desk in her luxurious office in Regent Street, London. At a smaller one near the window, her new assistant, Caroline Gerrard — slim, pretty, blonde-haired — was busy setting out her equipment. The sleek, shiny hands of the gold and ebony electric wall clock stood at nine-thirty.

This was Carol's first morning on her new job, in her new world. Only a few weeks before, she'd said goodbye to Shelburne College and to her schooldays. Launching out now into this novel, exhilarating existence, she felt thrilled, excited, supremely happy and confident. For, even before the end of her last term at Shelburne, she'd had contact with her brilliant young employer; and she was serenely content in the knowledge that her future couldn't be in cleverer or more capable hands.

She stole a glance at the detective now. Victoria was busy sorting through her mail — her dark eyes glowing eagerly, her pale, slender, crimson-tipped fingers briskly efficient. Presently she looked up with a wise little smile.

'Ah, Caroline — this looks like our first case, my dear!' She waved a typewritten letter. 'An old friend of mine, Professor Lynch, wants us to go down to Esher, in Surrey; he's staying at Claygate Farm, near there.'

Carol's eyes widened.

'What's it about, Miss Lincoln? I mean . . . is it a murder?'

Victoria chuckled.

'No — merely a mysterious thief at work. The Professor has his famous collection of curios and antiques at the farm — and they're disappearing from a locked room one by one! Methinks we'd better get down there right away, Carol. Ring up the garage, will you? And ask them to bring my car round. Here's the number . . . '

★   ★   ★

As Victoria Lincoln knocked on the cottage door something fluttered past her head with a menacing squawk. Then the dark-haired youth who opened the door said: 'Kim! Kim — come here at once!'

He flushed as he saw the detective smiling at him. 'Isn't Kim awful? He keeps opening his cage door and . . . I — er, did you wish to see someone?'

On the trellis, well out of reach, perched the jackdaw, a gleam of mischief in its bright beady eyes.

'We're looking for Claygate Farm,' explained Victoria. 'Your jackdaw seems a little suspicious!'

'Take no notice of Kim, ma'am. He's been a proper devil just lately. You're at Claygate Farm now. At least, this is the cottage — the farm proper is just a few minutes' walk away. I'm going there myself. I'll show you.'

'I'm greatly obliged,' rejoined Miss Lincoln, glancing at a tall, powerfully-built boy who'd just strolled on to the porch. 'Perhaps we'd better introduce ourselves.'

She handed over her card.

'Lady detective, eh? I bet the old Professor's sent for you to solve the mystery of his vanishing valuables. Am I right?' Kim's owner looked up expectantly.

'Bull's-eye first time, sonny. What is your name?'

'Tom Derry.' He shot a quick, appraising glance at Carol, who smiled back pertly. 'This is Johnny Briggs. Our parents are farmers, too — but they've sent us here to Farmer Dawson because they think we'll learn the business better under a stranger.'

Johnny shrugged, hitched up his trousers.

'I hate the blinking job!' he growled. 'I wanted to be an actor, but Dad wouldn't hear of it.'

On the way to the farm Caroline sympathised.

'If you really have the stage in your blood, Johnny — you'll end up there one day. What's your line?'

'Comedy, conjuring, drama . . . anything that's going, Miss. Ploughing fields and milking cows is my idea of sheer hard labour.'

Victoria asked:

'Can you boys tell us anything about

these mysterious thefts? How long has Professor Lynch been here, for instance?'

'About three months, Ma'am,' Tom said. 'He told us several attempts had been made to burgle his house in London — that's why he moved all his valuables down here and rented rooms off Farmer Dawson.'

'The whole thing seems very puzzling,' commented Victoria. 'The Professor tells me he locks the room where his collection is, every time he leaves it. He's the only one with a key — yet rings and pendants and such-like keep disappearing as if by magic!'

They turned in at the farmhouse gate. As they walked up the red gravel drive, Farmer Dawson spotted them and opened the door. He was sturdy, grey-haired, fresh-faced, one of the old school of countrymen — hard-bitten, shrewd, and a little aggressive. His deep blue eyes were unwavering as he stared at Victoria Lincoln, then at Carol.

The detective held out her card.

'I think the Professor is expecting us, Mr. Dawson. This is my assistant, Miss Gerrard.'

The farmer nodded.

'Must say I'm glad to see you, ladies. It's about time something was done about these thefts. I'd never have let those rooms to Lynch if I could have foreseen this. You'd best see him right away — he's in his study at the end of the hall. Show them the way, Tom.'

They went down the hall.

A white-haired, scholarly-looking gentleman emerged from one of the rooms and advanced to greet them.

'Thank goodness you're here, Miss Lincoln!' he said as they shook hands warmly. 'Ah . . . so this is the assistant you were telling me about? Miss Gerrard, I believe?' The old man took Carol's hand, patted it. 'A lovely-looking child, Miss Lincoln — lovely indeed! If she grows up to be as clever as you, then she'll make a name for herself all right!'

Caroline blushed, though her blue eyes twinkled roguishly.

'Thank you, sir,' she murmured. She caught Victoria's sly wink. 'I intend to model myself on Miss Lincoln — in everything.'

'Well spoken, my dear!' Professor Lynch laughed, then suddenly his face changed. 'But — let's get to business. Ladies . . . I'm worried to death over my treasures. All my most valuable rings and brooches are being taken. Please come in and I'll tell you what's been happening.'

They went into the study, sat down. The Professor went on: 'Since I 'phoned you this morning, Miss Lincoln, there's been another robbery — a unique cameo brooch from my collection of Eastern curios. The room where I keep my treasures was locked — I'll swear to it. There's no windows to it, no other means of getting in . . . yet my brooch disappeared. It's — it's uncanny! It's terrible! What can we do?'

'Just a minute, sir.' Victoria made a few notes in her book. 'It seems to me the first thing we'll have to establish is, that there is really only one key to that room! Now — how can we do that? Can you give me — '

The Professor broke in: 'Well, listen; when I first took these rooms Dawson didn't know anything about my treasures.

I'd been here a month before they arrived from London. Now during the second week of my stay I accidentally locked myself out of the room where my collection is now — it's a spring lock — a Yale. Surely if there'd been another key, Dawson would have produced it to let me in?'

'No doubt he would. Well, what happened?'

'He said he was sorry, but there was only the one key, the one he'd given me and which I'd left inside when I'd come out and pulled the door to. So we actually had to break open the door — and we also broke the lock in the process. I had to pay for the door being repaired, and for a new lock. I was there when the plumber fitted it in. There's two keys, as you know, Miss Lincoln, with every new lock of that type — and the plumber handed both to me when he'd finished. You see? I'm the only one with keys to that door!'

'You're sure you have both keys now, Professor?'

'Absolutely. Here — look.' He held out his key ring, pointing to two new Yale keys. At a glance, the detective could see they were identical.

They went out, Lynch leading the way. In the hall he started violently, his hand gripping Victoria's arm. 'Listen! What was that?'

From a room almost opposite had come a strange fluttering sound, followed by a splintering crash!

In a second Miss Lincoln and Carol were racing for the door, Professor Lynch at their heels. The Professor soon produced his keys.

Victoria Lincoln saw a long, pleasantly-furnished room; the mellow afternoon sunlight streaming through the door revealed the valuable curios and bric-a-brac arranged on tables and shelves flanking the panelled walls. The only ventilation was a small fanlight set high in the far wall. What had caused the Professor's exclamation was an Oriental vase lying shattered on the floor!

With trembling hands Lynch bent to collect the fragments. Caroline snapped on the lights, and Victoria took a quick glance round. In the middle of the right hand wall was a cupboard door. She went over, pulled it open. Nothing there but dusty, empty shelves . . .

Her thoughts flew to Tom Derry's jack-daw, and the peculiar fluttering sound they'd heard. Certainly, nothing much bigger than Kim could have entered through that fanlight. There was no other way into the room save through the door — which most definitely had been locked . . .

Victoria Lincoln spoke tersely.

'Check your collection, Professor. Make sure nothing else is missing.'

Shaking his head and muttering, the Professor did so. Meanwhile, Caroline scrutinised the floor. Suddenly she bent to retrieve something lying under a nearby table. Swiftly she passed it to Miss Lincoln, who nodded meaningfully as she slipped the small object in her pocket.

At that moment there came a horrified shout from Lynch.

'My diamond ring — my solitaire diamond!'

There was a rush of feet up the hall. Farmer Dawson, Tom and Johnny came running in.

'What's wrong now?' demanded the farmer. 'I heard the crash, then — ' He saw the Professor's white, strained face.

'Don't tell me there's been another theft?'

The Professor was pointing to the velvet bed of a small showcase. A space in the centre was blank.

'It was there half an hour ago!' he cried chokingly. 'Now it's gone! It's incredible . . .'

The detective glanced sharply at the two speechless boys. Dark-haired Tom Derry looked puzzled and rather excited; Johnny Briggs was very pale, his hands tightly clenched.

'This is getting past a joke!' barked Farmer Dawson. 'My folks have lived at Claygate Farm for hundreds of years and never has a breath of scandal been attached to it — till now!' He frowned across at the boys. 'You'd best get back to work, you two.'

The boys backed reluctantly towards the door. Dawson turned to Victoria. 'Found any clues yet, Miss Lincoln?'

Victoria smiled. 'We've a tough job this time, sir. Looks like an invisible thief has to be caught!'

'Invisible?' The farmer's brows were creased.

'Apparently; since the only way in and out of this room, apart from the door, is

76

that fanlight — a mere six inches wide! However, I'll do my best to find the thief.'

Professor Lynch came forward, rubbing his hands agitatedly.

'That jackdaw, ladies — Kim, they call it — it belongs to Tom Derry . . . it's always escaping from its cage and flying about the place. That could get in through the fanlight!'

Farmer Dawson said:

'Aye — I've thought of Kim once or twice. Jackdaws will fly off with anything that sparkles, Miss Lincoln. I never liked young Derry having it.'

'It's an idea, gentlemen, responded Victoria. 'For the moment, we'll take a good look round. Lock the door very carefully, Professor, and don't let the keys out of your sight.'

Beckoning to Caroline, the detective walked thoughtfully down the hall towards the rear of the building. Next to the kitchen door, another stood slightly ajar. It contained a desk, table, and leather armchair — this much Victoria saw in passing. Obviously the farmer's private room. It contained something else that started a peculiar train of thought in Victoria's mind; there was a huge safe planted across one corner . . .

They left the farmhouse, strolled quietly through the field at the rear. Presently voices reached their ears; youthful voices raised indignantly.

Rounding a hedge, they came across Tom and Johnny arguing heatedly.

'Hello! What's the trouble?' Miss Lincoln asked.

Both boys turned, their faces flushed. Tom said:

'Johnny's hinting that all jackdaws are thieves!'

'What are you suggesting, Johnny?' Victoria demanded.

'Why, that it's quite possible it's Kim who's stealing the Professor's things. It *is* possible, isn't it, Miss Gerrard?'

Caroline laughed, though her eyes were grave.

'Kim? Surely he's safely locked away in his cage at the cottage. You *did* lock him up, Tom?'

'Certainly. I caught him just after you knocked on the door. Remember?'

Miss Lincoln nodded.

'I do. Anyway, just to make sure, and to satisfy Johnny — we'll have a look, eh?'

They accompanied the boys back to the cottage. In the hall Tom Derry gave a startled cry.

'Kim! He's gone!'

The cage door was open, with no sign of Kim. An open window near the bend in the stairs completed the story.

Johnny's voice was triumphant. 'There! What did I tell you? Kim is the thief all right!'

'Well, *I* don't believe it,' said Tom. 'Miss Lincoln, what's your idea?'

'I don't think it's Kim, either.' Victoria Lincoln spoke emphatically. 'I've never yet met a jackdaw smart enough to select the rarest gems from a collection of valuables. Anyway — how on earth does he get out of his cage?'

Tom shook his head in bewilderment. 'Heaven only knows. Have a look yourself, ma'am. There's a really strong catch to the cage-door. I can't see how he can possibly lift that pin.'

They went over, made a careful examination.

'As you say, it seems barely possible,' Victoria announced presently. 'Still, we must face facts. Kim *does* get out — so the only thing to do is strengthen that catch. By the way, Tom . . . how long have you had him?'

'Oh, about — let's see . . . three months, ma'am. Farmer Dawson gave him to me. I think Kim's a grand old boy. I'm very proud of him!'

'*Farmer Dawson* gave him to you?' Carol's voice held a puzzled note.

The detective and her assistant exchanged significant glances. Victoria said softly:

'I see. Well — he won't have flown very far, Tom. We'll find him, don't you worry. Now I think you lads had better get back to work — or Farmer Dawson will be chasing the four of us!'

As she spoke the detective's fingers closed tightly on the object Caroline had picked up in Professor Lynch's room of curios. It was a black quill feather that could have fallen from a jackdaw's wing!

★   ★   ★

That evening Victoria Lincoln gave Caroline her instructions, then went walking through the fields at the rear of the farm. Chickens clucked and scurried out of her way; a cow regarded her with large, enquiring eyes over a gate. In such peaceful, rustic surroundings the thought of crime seemed unbelievable.

Certainly, all the evidence seemed to point to Kim. Still, there were other peculiar facts, too. For instance, how did the bird escape from its cage? And why had Farmer Dawson said he objected to it, when he himself had given the bird to Tom?

Past the stables, Victoria paused, looked back. The redbrick farmhouse, mellow in the evening sunlight and cosily covered with ivy, stood at the far side of the meadow on a slight hill. Hard to believe that here a mysterious thief was at work, flaunting all precautions, entering and leaving as and when he liked!

Suddenly the detective stiffened. Her sensitive ears had detected a faint sound — a rustling in the hedge close by. She stood motionless, watching and waiting.

The rustling came again. Then Victoria noticed the long grass bordering the hedge shaking slightly as something moved through it.

Quick as a flash Victoria sprang; there was a shrill, protesting squawk and a frightened fluttering.

In her firm grasp wriggled Kim, the errant jackdaw! Something gleamed in its yellow beak. Victoria had just noticed it when a quick step made her wheel round. Caroline Gerrard walked up swiftly, her eyes gleaming.

'I was just having a scout round, Miss Lincoln. I see you've nabbed Kim, eh? And with the swag on him! That's one of the Professor's trinkets in his beak, isn't it?'

'You've pretty sharp eyes, Carol!'

With a swift movement Victoria Lincoln extracted the cameo brooch from Kim's beak — the one that had been stolen that very morning!'

'Well, thank goodness the mystery's been solved at last,' exclaimed Carol. 'Let's go and tell Farmer Dawson right away.'

'Not so fast, my dear. I've a few other

ideas I want to try out — and I need your help!'

'Okay, Miss Lincoln! What d'you want me to do?'

'I want to know everything you've discovered up to now, for a start! You remember me saying I've known many a jackdaw in my time that could talk almost as good as a trained parrot? Well . . . did you find out if Kim can talk?'

'Well — Tom says he's only ever heard him say one word — 'bread'. When he's hungry he squawks that sometimes.'

Kim's bright, beady eyes flicked round as he wriggled in Victoria's hand. A hoarse sound came from his throat as, hearing the word, he opened his beak.

'Well, that *could* be taken for bread, I suppose,' said Victoria. 'Has Farmer Dawson ever heard him?

'Yes. Tom says he's often tried to teach Kim other words.'

'Fine. Now tell me if you ever did any amateur theatricals at school, Carol.'

Surprised at the abrupt change in the conversation, but only too willing nevertheless to discuss her favourite hobby,

Caroline spoke eagerly as they walked slowly back to the farm.

As they neared the stables Kim became suddenly very wide-awake and excited, struggling to get free and flapping his wings. Victoria Lincoln halted, her brows drawn together in a frown.

Suddenly she noticed a trace of recent footprints on the muddy ground; the tracks of someone who wore narrow, pointed shoes. Surely such shoes were out of place on a farm?

Caroline followed her pointing finger.

'They lead into that old stable, Miss Lincoln — and it's only used for tipping rubbish. Should we take a look?'

'Yes!' said Victoria. 'Come on!'

They poked about for quite a while without success: but the detective noted that each time they went near a pile of rotting straw in one corner Kim became doubly excited. Her eyes glinted as she grabbed a stick, scattering the straw aside.

A startled gasp broke from Carol.

'Miss Lincoln — look at that!'

Beneath the pile was a heap of cameo rings and brooches — broken and twisted almost beyond recognition!

Victoria Lincoln whistled softly; then she bent, gathered up the battered trinkets, put them in her bag.

'I think this is where Kim made his find, Carol. It was pecking round here for tidbits and found that brooch.' She straightened, her eyes narrowing. 'This little find just about clinches my theory, my dear. Now listen: I'm going to call a general meeting tonight, for eight o'clock in the Professor's curio room. I'm leaving Kim in your charge till then — because I want you there with him. Understand? So put him in his cage and don't let him out of your sight.'

Caroline nodded. As they walked towards the farm Victoria carefully outlined her plans for the meeting; she didn't stop talking till she was satisfied that her young assistant had everything quite clear.

'That's it, then,' she concluded. 'Meantime, I've business to do in the village. I'll call for you at the cottage about a quarter to eight.'

At the farm she told Farmer Dawson to

85

get everyone together in the curio room for eight o'clock.

'I've an idea we're going to catch this thief tonight, sir — and clear Kim into the bargain!'

'I'll be more than glad to get the confounded business settled,' growled the farmer.

He returned to his books, while Victoria Lincoln made her way to the village. There, she called in at the police station and had a long chat with the inspector.

A few minutes after eight that evening, a silent little group assembled in Professor Lynch's curio room. Farmer Dawson, his rugged face sternly clouded, sat in a high-backed chair, puffing solidly at his pipe. Professor Lynch stood nearby, while guarding the door was a silent village constable. Facing them, her back to an exquisite Venetian screen, stood Victoria Lincoln, holding the mischievous Kim firmly in her arms. Tom Derry and Johnny Briggs lounged against the wall.

The detective glanced round quickly, then began:

'I promised the Professor I'd try and

solve the mystery of his vanishing trinkets, gentlemen — and I think I've done it! The first thing that struck me as being suspicious was this: that only cameo rings and brooches were being stolen. There were other gems, other valuables, some of far greater value — but only anything containing a cameo was being taken. That is, until this afternoon; when, for the first time, an ordinary diamond ring was missing.

'Now this peculiar fact set me off right away on a line of investigation. How would it be, I thought, if the thief wasn't after the trinkets for their own value — but for something that maybe one of them contained?'

Victoria Lincoln held up her hand.

'Recently, Professor, you purchased at an auction sale, the entire collection of an elderly gentleman named McKesson, who was something of an eccentric. It was his wife who ordered the sale, after his sudden death. She didn't know that a great many of the old-fashioned, cameo rings and brooches in the collection had cavities behind their embossed enamel signets — and that in these cavities

McKesson had secreted several priceless diamonds!'

Somewhere a boot scraped uneasily on the stone floor. Looking round, sternly, Victoria went on:

'Nevertheless, there was a notorious London jewel thief named Nips Dapier who did know about this — and he was there at the auction when you made your purchase, Professor. That's why he made so many attempts to burgle your house.' Miss Lincoln paused dramatically. 'And that's why he followed you down here and continued with his efforts to rob you!'

Farmer Dawson laughed harshly.

'A jewel thief, on Claygate Farm? Don't be childish, madam! The whole thing is fantastic!'

'I agree,' said Victoria quietly. 'Nips dared not reveal himself openly, because he knew both I and the police were on his track. He hid in the deserted stable on your farm, Mr. Dawson — and waited till the cameo trinkets were brought to him by his accomplice.'

'Ah — the jackdaw, without a doubt!' cried Lynch.

'Not so,' snapped the detective. 'I admit this crafty accomplice staged things so that everything pointed to Kim being the culprit: Truth will out, however! As soon as I suspected the hand of Dapier in this I got in touch with the local police. Dapier was arrested an hour ago, leaving the village in his car — with a small fortune in diamonds in his pockets. To make things easier for himself, he's already revealed the name of his accomplice!'

There was a sudden scrape as Dawson's chair shot back. Next second he was on his feet.

'He has, eh? Well, let's get busy and nab him. Who is it, Miss Lincoln?'

He was making for the door, but the constable barred the way.

'Take it easy, sir — Miss Lincoln hasn't finished yet.'

Dawson stood scowling darkly. Professor Lynch said:

'But if it wasn't the jackdaw — how on earth did this accomplice get in here?'

Vicky Lincoln smiled grimly.

'I think we'll let Kim answer that question, Professor. You see — he can talk quite well . . . jackdaws do, sometimes. Kim was hopping about on the fanlight up there one time he was free, and actually saw Dapier's accomplice coming in. Now then, Kim — speak up, old boy!'

The detective's eyes were glued now on Farmer Dawson, whose glance flickered quickly to the cupboard arrangement in the right-hand wall. Then came a throaty, evil-sounding squawk.

'*Dawson, Dawson, old Farmer Dawson . . . came through the wall — the wall — ha-h-h . . .* '

The farmer made a dive for the door, but the constable was like a granite block barring the way. He grabbed Dawson's arms and next second handcuffs gleamed on the farmer's wrists.

Miss Lincoln had yet another surprise. She yanked aside the screen before which she'd been standing, and there stood her young assistant, Caroline Gerrard!

★ ★ ★

Over supper Victoria Lincoln made things a little plainer. 'I became suspicious of old

Dawson when he told us he objected to Kim — when all the time he'd given the bird to Tom; purposely, of course, so that he'd have something to blame, when he started stealing the Professor's rings. He didn't know the diamonds were hidden inside, though! He'd been hard pressed for money for some time, and he finally agreed to Dapier's suggestion that he should rob his guest. Dawson it was who kept letting Kim out of his cage; no one would suspect a jackdaw that was never free!

'Another thing that made me suspect him was his safe. An honest man, I reckoned, would have insisted that the Professor's valuables be locked away securely as soon as they started disappearing. Naturally, that wouldn't have suited Dawson; if they'd vanished from his safe, then there'd only have been him for it.

'He took the cameo brooch this morning and hid it in the stable for Dapier to collect; but he'd also let Kim out; and Kim, poking about there, had it first! I suppose Dawson realised that, when Miss Gerrard and I arrived, he wouldn't have quite such a free hand. So this afternoon he took a diamond ring for himself. While he was in there he flapped a magazine about to imitate a bird's wings, and dropped one of Kim's feathers on the floor. No one can say he wasn't thorough!

'When I told him to call the meeting this evening he knew things were getting hot, so he contacted Dapier and told him to get going. This time, however, we stepped in first.

'The one thing that puzzled me most was: how on earth did Dawson get into the curio room? I was satisfied he hadn't a key. The only thing in that room that could possibly have concealed an entrance was that cupboard in the wall. Of course we know now that it's an old serving hatch, used years ago when the curio room was used for dining. It lets into the kitchen — and that's how Dawson entered and left.

'The point was — how could we trap him? Actually, it was talking to Johnny Briggs that gave me the idea. When he said he was dead set on being an actor, my assistant told him that he'd end up on the stage one day, if he was keen enough!

'That made me think that she knew something about the stage; and when I questioned her, I found she'd been a shining light in her school Dramatic Society, that she was something of a ventriloquist — and that she was quite handy at imitating the noises made by various birds and animals.

'I realised that, at the meeting, Dawson might try and bluster things out. My plan was, to scare him into giving himself away. That's why Miss Gerrard and I staged our little scene. Apparently it was good enough to unnerve old Dawson completely. Congrats, Carol, my dear! You put on a great show!'

'I think you're a marvel, Miss Lincoln!' breathed Tom Derry.

'I think they *both* are!' Johnny asserted fervently.

Professor Lynch raised his glass.

'I'll drink to that, gentlemen!'

Victoria Lincoln and Caroline smiled their thanks.

4

No Shred of Evidence

A mile and a half through the little town of Radstock, in Somerset, they came to wide green gates fronting a tree-lined driveway. A crested board fixed on the wall bore the words:

ST. HILDA'S COLLEGE
FOR GIRLS.
Headmistress:
MARION LAWRENCE, M.A.

Miss Victoria Lincoln, the private detective, swung her car on to the grass verge and turned off the engine. Her young assistant, Caroline Gerrard, patted her short blonde curls beneath her hat and slid from her seat. Victoria Lincoln followed, locking the car doors.

As they walked up the drive Caroline said:

'What a lovely place, Miss Lincoln. Beautiful lawns, a marvellous house . . . look! Can you imagine anyone in their senses running away from it?'

'You're jumping ahead a little, Carol!' Victoria smiled at her youthful assistant. 'We're not sure yet that Mr. Baxter did run away. That's what we're down here to find out.'

They were shown immediately to Miss Lawrence's study.

'How are, you, Marion?' Victoria asked, as they shook hands warmly. 'I'm very glad you sent for me. It must have been over a year since we met!'

Miss Lawrence was tall, pale . . . she looked dreadfully tired.

'I do hope you'll be able to help us, Vicky. Poor Mr. Baxter disappearing like that — it just seems to have turned everything upside down.' She glanced quickly at Caroline. 'And who is the young lady?'

'Ah, this is Carol Gerrard, Marion. An ex-Shelburne girl . . . she came to me a couple of months ago when she finished at the college.'

'That's so interesting!' murmured Miss

Lawrence. 'Now — this business of Mr. Baxter . . . he was our music teacher, you understand, Vicky. Well liked by the girls, extremely quiet and reserved — his life seemed to be wrapped up in his music and his house.'

'He lived nearby?'

'Yes — you can see his place from here. Look . . . ' She beckoned them to the window. Across the playing fields, nestling behind a coppice of cypress trees, they saw a trim little house gravel-washed a pale green. 'The first I heard about him being missing was at eleven o'clock, three nights ago . . . when his housekeeper, Mrs. Simon, came running over very agitatedly to enquire if he was here. He'd left about eight, she said, saying he was slipping down to the corner to post a letter, then to have a stroll, but that he'd be back for his supper, which he always ate at nine o'clock.'

Victoria said softly:

'So — at eight on Wednesday evening last Edsel Baxter left home and vanished into thin air? No sign or trace has been found of him since?'

'That's it, exactly. Now — d'you think you can help us, Vicky?'

'Well, there doesn't seem a great deal to go on. Can you tell me anything about Mr. Baxter?'

'That's the trouble — I can't! I know so little of him. He'd never taught in England before; he'd been in France for ages, but what he did there other than music teaching, of course, I never learned. His credentials were absolutely first rate, I can vouch for that; and both his conduct and his work here bore them out fully.'

'I see. Was he married? Had he any friends? Did he do any entertaining at his house?'

'No. Apart from his housekeeper he lived alone. And his only friend, to my knowledge, was Squire Hargrave, his brother-in-law — you'd pass his place just out of town on the way here . . . a rambling, old-fashioned, ivy-covered house.'

Miss Lincoln jumped up.

'All right, Marion . . . we'll take the case on and we'll do our very best for you. I realise the publicity is none too good for St. Hilda's. Come on, Carol, my dear — our first step is to interview this Mrs. Simon.'

The housekeeper saw them coming as they walked up the garden path. As they stepped on to the portico she opened the door. She was tall, angular, with a vinegary eye — she stood back and beckoned them in, making an effort to smile.

'You'll be Miss Lincoln, I reckon — the famous detective? Miss Lawrence told me to be expecting you.'

'That's right. This is my assistant, Miss Gerrard. I suppose you're Mrs. Simon?'

'I am. Will you please come in?'

They followed her into the living room. Caroline stood in the background while Victoria went near the fire with Mrs. Simon. Dabbing her eyes with a rather dirty handkerchief, the housekeeper produced a letter from her apron pocket, held it out to Victoria.

'Here, Miss Lincoln — read this. It came by the afternoon post — barely an hour ago. I don't know what to make of it! It's — it's terrible . . . '

Her pale face creased as she plied her handkerchief. Victoria opened the single sheet of notepaper, glanced across at Carol, then read aloud:

'*Dear Mrs. Simon,*

Things are very bad with me and I've decided to end my life. I intend to do it in such way that my body never will be found.

I cannot explain here, but I am in terrible debt and the bank has refused me further credit. I am sorry to leave you like this but it is the only way. If you show this letter to Elmer Hargrave I'm sure he will find you a place.

I wish you good luck and the best of health.

Edsel B. Baxter.'

Victoria Lincoln folded the letter slowly, put it in her pocket.

'I'll keep this, with your kind permission, Mrs. Simon. No doubt, of course, that it's his writing?'

'No doubt at all, Miss Lincoln. He wrote it all right.'

'H'm'm.' Victoria told Mrs. Simon to sit down, but she herself remained standing.

'Now will you give us all the details, Mrs. Simon? Just the facts as you know them.'

'I will indeed. I've been with poor Mr. Baxter this last eight months and I know him pretty well. Up till — till three nights ago he'd never stopped away once. Then that evening,' — she spoke slowly, flavouring each word — 'that evening about eight he called into the kitchen from his study door. He said, 'Just taking a stroll into the village, Mrs. Simon. Won't be long'. I heard the front door slam and that was the last I heard of him.'

'You didn't actually see him go, then?'

'No, miss. I told you — '

'Certainly, certainly. Just a small point, Mrs. Simon. Might be an important detail just the same. Very well. Carry on.'

'Well, nine o'clock came and I prepared his supper. No Mr. Baxter. Half past nine, ten . . . no Mr. Baxter. I 'phoned up to Squire Hargrave, the next house down the lane; he's Mr. Baxter's brother-in-law and they were old school friends . . . but no, he wasn't there and hadn't been there that evening. I didn't know anywhere else he might be. So I ran across to the school and saw Miss Lawrence — but she hadn't seen him all evening, either. Well, I didn't know what to do. I stayed up till midnight, then had a look round and went to bed.'

'I see. Now — did he take anything with him when he left? You didn't see him, you say — but you'll know if — '

She cut in. 'Not a single stitch — he never even took a hat or coat. I've been through his clothes. I know everything he had to wear and it's all there. He went out in his grey suit — that's all he took.'

Miss Lincoln nodded slowly.

'Well, Mrs. Simon, it looks like a plain case of suicide — but until we find the body we can't really proceed. No doubt the police have worked on that angle — there's those old waterlogged quarries at St. Clair, for instance, and the lake at the top of Wyandotte Wood. One or two places can be searched. Routine, of course — though I'm not hopeful. From the sound of this letter I imagine he'd laid his plans very carefully indeed. By the way — have you a photo of him? I'd very much — '

'There's several lying around.' Mrs. Simon

went to a bureau near the fireplace, rummaged in a drawer. 'Here — one he had taken in his new riding outfit, a few weeks ago. That's the latest, I think . . . '

Victoria took it, studied it intently. Caroline came across, looked over her shoulder. They saw a shortish, plump individual with piercing dark eyes, thick Vandyke beard, and side-whiskers. The close-fitting riding trousers accentuated his stoutness.

Victoria looked up at Mrs. Simon.

'Lived well, by the look of this. His worries didn't affect his appetite, did they?'

'Mr. Baxter always ate well, Miss Lincoln. Always very keen on exercise, he was, too. That is, until his accident about a year ago. He twisted his leg somehow, so he told me — and he's walked with a limp ever since. That's the reason he put on weight — missing his exercise, he said.'

Miss Lincoln interrupted her by handing back the photo.

'A very interesting picture, Mrs. Simon. Before we go, I'd like you to tell us something of Mr. Baxter's home life; his pleasures, how he amused himself, what kind of man he was about the house — did he strike you as being perfectly normal or did he have any peculiar habits ... you know. Things like that. Personal details ...'

Caroline found her heart was beating a little faster than usual as she watched and listened as Victoria, tense and ever-watchful, skilfully cross-examined the tearful housekeeper.

'His pleasures weren't many, nor big, I reckon. He liked his pipe and a good book as much as anything. He went visiting with his sister and brother-in-law a goodish bit. He and Squire Hargrave went to high school together, so he told me — they're life-long friends. A quieter man than Edsel Baxter you couldn't wish for.' She stared at her hands, her lips drawn up in a bunch. Then, as an afterthought, she added: 'He had his funny ways, I suppose, like everyone else.'

Victoria's voice was eager. 'He had, eh? How d'you mean, Mrs. Simon?'

'Well — I always make myself a cup of tea early morning, while I'm dusting and laying the fires and so on; and one time I thought he'd like one; so I took a cup upstairs, thinking it'd be a nice surprise for him. When he saw me he started telling me off something awful. 'Goodness gracious', I said to him, 'you take a week's notice, Mr. Baxter, if that's how you feel,' I said. But no. He smoothed it over, just said he was real touchy about anyone coming in his bedroom while he was there. He apologised, so we left it at that. He had no more tea in bed.'

Watching her, Victoria mentioned another point.

'You say he twisted his leg one time, Mrs. Simon — around a year ago, you think? What happened exactly?'

'I don't know exactly, Miss Lincoln. Far as I know he did it over at Mr. Hargrave's. He told me he'd been visiting there one night, and he'd had a fall. That's what started his limp, he said.'

'Was it noticeable?'

'It was indeed. Something like this, it was.' Mrs. Simon went across the room and back, dragging her left leg.

'I see, Mrs. Simon. Now about that morning when you took him the early cup of tea. Did you notice anything peculiar about him?'

Caroline suddenly felt her scalp prickle. Had Miss Lincoln hit on something . . . ?

The housekeeper paused, her brows drawn.

'Nothing peculiar, miss — no. It just seemed to me what a lot thinner he looked in his night things, that's all. Clothes *do* make such a difference to a man. Real slim he looked, Miss Lincoln. I remember thinking at the time: all his walking about his room must've been having some effect after all.'

'Walking about his room?' Victoria's voice held a high note of interest. 'You haven't mentioned that, Mrs. Simon. What was all that about?'

'Well, I suppose it was his way of keeping fit. He did it mostly when I was cleaning up early mornings, sometimes he did it at night. About ten minutes a day he'd spend at it — up and down, up and down, across his room.'

'You knew, naturally, that it was Mr. Baxter up there — walking up and down, over your head? He, and no one else?'

'Good gracious! Why, of course it was Mr. Baxter! Who else could it be? There was nobody else here — just him and me . . .'

'Certainly, Mrs. Simon. It's just a similar point to the other. You didn't see him walking around his room — you just *heard* him. That's enough though, isn't it? You'd know him by the limp — apart from anything else. Remember? The left foot dragging . . . ?'

Mrs. Simon suddenly sat bolt upright, her eyes wide with surprise. Victoria spoke softly:

'Think. Mrs. Simon. Think! You're down here dusting and cleaning and laying the fire. You hear the footsteps over your head, walking up and down, up and down. They go like this.' She paced the room again, limping. Mrs. Simon found her tongue.

'Well, that's an extraordinary thing, Miss Lincoln! Now I come to think of it, Mr. Baxter *didn't* limp when he was taking his exercise in his room!' Her face bore an expression of complete bewilderment. 'I can hear him now, almost. He didn't limp at all! What d'you make of it?'

She paused, her face white and

strained. Caroline's heart thumped wildly as Victoria Lincoln watched the housekeeper, not replying for a moment. Mrs. Simon went on quickly:

'But it *must* have been him! How could anybody have got in morning after morning and done the walking? And why should they? It must've been him! If it wasn't — well, *who was it?*'

'I don't know yet, Mrs. Simon. Nevertheless I *will* know — be sure of that. Anyway, you've been very helpful, and we're grateful. We'd like a look around the house, if you could manage . . . '

The housekeeper stood up, swept towards the door.

'No trouble, miss — if you'll follow me.'

On the ground floor was the room Baxter had used as his study. A small, rather dark apartment; furnished principally with weighty old-fashioned volumes and a large roll-top desk. All the drawers of this were unlocked, and empty. At a sign from Victoria, Caroline yanked them all out. She pulled one so hard that it shot out completely. Something fluttered to the floor — a handbill or something similar, that had fallen behind the drawer and wedged there. Miss Lincoln retrieved it, glanced at it and put it in her pocket.

They went upstairs. Here the rooms were by no means so impressively furnished. In fact, the bedroom about which Baxter had been so particular was almost commonplace. The other rooms held nothing of any interest. In the ceiling above the attic landing there was a hatchway. Victoria could just reach it by balancing precariously on the balustrade. Mrs. Simon watched impassively, her hands folded in front of her.

'We never use that,' she offered. 'Never seen it open while I've been here.'

Miss Lincoln jumped down.

'I won't rest till I've seen inside. Find a pair of steps, Mrs. Simon — won't take a minute . . . '

Clicking her teeth, the housekeeper moved off into a little anteroom, to return presently with a small stepladder. Victoria reared it, climbed up, and pushed it open, then struck a match, and disappeared into the hole. They heard her scraping about; after a moment she came down again, smiling.

'Nothing at all — you're right, Mrs. Simon. Nothing but rafters and cobwebs and inches of dust all over. Sorry to have bothered you, but it's best to make sure.'

They went downstairs, washed their hands. Victoria said:

'You'll be hearing from us again in a day or so, Mrs. Simon. In the meantime we'll pay a visit to Squire Hargrave. Which is the best way to get to his place?'

Mrs. Simon opened the back door.

'See?' she pointed. Across the fields they could make out the barns and granaries of Hargrave's farm, and his acres of plough and pasture land stretching away to the dark, sprawling blot that was Wyandotte Wood. 'Carry on down the lane when you leave here,' she went on. 'There's another gate like ours a mile or so down. That's his. You can't mistake it . . .'

They thanked her and departed. Walking down the drive Caroline said:

'Have you discovered anything, Miss Lincoln?'

Victoria smiled faintly.

'I think I know how Mr. Baxter disappeared, Carol. As for why — well, perhaps Squire Hargrave will help us there!'

'Then you don't think Mr. Baxter's killed himself?'

Victoria squeezed her young assistant's arm. 'You mustn't rush me, Carol!'

They entered the car; Miss Lincoln drove slowly down the lane.

* * *

Hargrave saw them walking along the muddy cart track towards his farmstead. As they forded the puddles of his rickyard he opened the front door.

'Well, ladies — and what can I do for you?'

Miss Lincoln handed him her card, introduced Caroline, and explained their business. Bowing slightly. Hargrave asked them inside.

As they followed him down the hall, Victoria made a quick decision about Hargrave. She'd recognised, in the farmer's arrogant manner, high nostrils and arched brows, the bullying, commanding type; she saw a man who, by his aggressive pride, would be robbed of many of life's sweetest gifts. She saw — or thought she saw — one who, at a pinch, would not shrink from murder . . .

They followed him into a dark room that crouched beneath its low ceiling. Mrs. Hargrave sat by the fireside, knitting; and when Miss Lincoln nodded to her and said, 'How-de-do, madam,' she answered in a voice that was so indescribably weary, that Caroline looked at her keenly.

She felt uneasy when she saw that Mrs. Hargrave's eyes were red with weeping, that her face was strained, almost haggard with fatigue. Nevertheless, Carol told herself that, in her youth, she must have been very beautiful . . .

Later, they were to discover that the townsfolk said hard things about the way Hargrave treated his wife.

Now, Miss Lincoln looked across at the farmer.

'You know Edsel Baxter is still missing, sir?'

'Certainly. I 'phoned his place this morning, as I do every day. What d'you make of it?'

'Suicide, I imagine. He sent a note — '

111

'Note?' Hargrave's voice was cutting. 'Mrs. Simon never mentioned that! What was that, pray?'

Victoria told them. Mrs. Hargrave said suddenly:

'It's *not* suicide! Edsel wouldn't do that. He never was a coward. There wasn't a braver nor finer man alive than my brother. He — '

She caught her husband's eye. He was scowling at her fiercely.

'Why don't you hold your unlucky tongue?' he snapped. 'Your precious brother has gone now, and you — '

Her lips quivered.

'You talk like that about — '

He wouldn't let her finish.

'I'll attend to you later, Margaret.' She heard the threat in his words, groped for her knitting. He turned to the detective. 'Baxter was all right — certainly. We were at school together, I've nothing against him; but my wife carries on as though he was a saint!'

'You can't throw any light on how, or where, Baxter may have killed himself?' Victoria asked.

Hargrave spread his hands.

'How can I? There's drowning — he could've done that in several places in Wyandotte Wood, in the filled-in quarries. Of course he might've gone far away — it's impossible to say. All I know is, he's told his sister and I several times how hard up be was.' He stared down at his feet. ''Fraid that's all I can tell you, ladies . . . '

He moved towards the door and Victoria Lincoln, hating the man suddenly, nodded to Caroline. They walked out slowly, Hargrave banging the door behind them.

They crossed the rickyard in silence. Then presently Miss Lincoln jerked out:

'Wicked man, that . . . I don't like him, Carol.'

'Mr. Hargrave?'

'Yes.'

'Neither do I, Miss Lincoln. I don't like the way he looks at his wife. I bet he's not very kind to her!'

Victoria nodded, smiling thinly. At the gate they stood aside. A tall man wearing an old straw hat was leading a chestnut roan in from the lane. When he saw them he stopped, fumbling with the bridle. Miss Lincoln leaned on the gate.

'Hello, young man. Do you work here?'

'Yes, ma'am, that I do. My name's Renfrew — I'm Mr. Hargrave's stable man.' He paused, looking very uncomfortable. 'You want me?' he asked.

Victoria Lincoln said:

'Look: Mr. Baxter — you know Mr. Edsel Baxter, don't you? Well, he's missing from home, and we're making a few enquiries. Is there anything you know . . . that might help?'

As usual with such folk, Renfrew was very eager to give assistance; but all he could tell them was that Baxter had been a frequent visitor at the Hargraves' for as long as he'd worked there.

Victoria tried a new angle.

'Who d'you think he came to see — chiefly?' she asked. 'Mr. Hargrave — or his sister?'

Renfrew shuffled his feet. The knowing look that spread over his wide features was comical.

'They do say Mr. Edsel was very fond of his sister, ma'am. Brought her flowers and that, often. And when the boss rides to the market every week at Frome — why, he was in to dinner that day reg'lar so his sister should not be lonely. The boss is away all day, see, once a week — he doesn't get back till maybe one or two in the morning.'

'Rides to market, Renfrew? You mean . . . ?'

Renfrew patted the roan's neck.

'Yes, ma'am — on this horse here. He's rode her there an' back every week . . . this last ten months, anyhow.'

'Well, fancy that! Look: do you think Mr. Hargrave knew Mr. Baxter came to lunch here with his sister on the days he was away?'

'Can't say to that, ma'am. Me, I don't think the boss and Mrs. Hargrave get on that good. They do say he's a bit unkind to her, I — '

He stopped. Victoria saw his face redden, and turned. Hargrave was striding down the path, his face flushed, his eyes blazing. He came up shouting.

'Renfrew — get about your work, man! I don't pay you to stand gossiping.' He stood breathing heavily as the stable hand led the roan off. Then he turned to Victoria and Carol. 'Anything you want to know, *I'll* tell you. If you don't mind, ladies . . .'

Miss Lincoln snapped:

'We'll question whom we think fit, Mr. Hargrave. Have you anything else to say?'

'All right, all right — I admit I'm a little put out by all this business.' Hargrave avoided Victoria's cold scrutiny. Then he added: 'I've nothing else to tell you — nothing at all . . .'

Victoria nodded, then signed to Caroline. They went into the lane, not answering. They entered the car. Miss Lincoln trod on the starter. They heard the gate clang to as the car began rolling.

Victoria Lincoln drove slowly, hunched over the wheel. She spoke softly, her eyes narrowed.

'I'm beginning to think the strangest things about this affair, Carol. The most extraordinary things . . .'

Caroline said excitedly:

'Honestly, Miss Lincoln? You've found a clue?'

'Well, look at all the peculiar points that stand out. First: from that photo, it's obvious that Baxter's hands are long and slim — but the rest of him was all stoutness!

'Second: how scared he was of Mrs. Simon seeing him in his bedroom. He didn't mind her going in — but seeing him, oh no — he wouldn't have that.

'Third: her saying he looked thinner in his pyjamas.

'Fourth: Baxter's limp. Why should he lose it when he walks in his bedroom? Had he a magic carpet that cured him while he was on it? I don't think so!

'And lastly: in that attic, where there were inches of dust everywhere, there was just one spot that was clean. Yes — a little square just inside the trap door, where something had lain — very, very recently. Yet Mrs. Simon swore the attic was never used!'

She nodded several times, her lips pursed.

'Well, I don't see that we can *do* very much till Mr. Baxter's found — either alive or . . . dead,' Caroline said. 'D'you think — someone *murdered* him, Miss Lincoln?'

Miss Lincoln's voice was grim.

'I'll say this, Carol — if *this* one isn't a murder . . . I'm pretty sure the next one will be!'

Caroline thought about this for a while. They drove on in silence.

* * *

The following Thursday was market day at Frome. About eight a.m., Renfrew brought the roan, ready saddled, into the yard. A few minutes later Squire Hargrave came out and mounted. Renfrew watched his master ride off along the field path towards Wyandotte Wood; and that was the last time anyone saw him alive. Mrs. Hargrave expected him back around two o'clock the following morning, but he did not return.

Renfrew arrived as usual at five a.m. and was surprise to see the roan, standing in the yard, still saddled and nibbling at a rick; for he knew Hargrave was proud of the horse and always stabled it carefully whatever the hour of his return.

Then around eight o' clock Mrs. Hargrave came into the dairy.

'Renfrew — have you seen my husband this morning?'

'I — why no, ma'am. His horse was in the yard when I came at five . . . I thought he'd be in bed . . . '

She shook her head.

'He hasn't been in, Renfrew. Perhaps he's fallen from the saddle. Take the mare and ride back through the wood.'

'Yes, ma'am. Right away.'

★ ★ ★

Renfrew saw nothing till he was trotting up the slope leading to Wynberg's Grove, in the deepest and leafiest corner of the small forest. Then, fifty yards past the woodman's hut, he saw his master.

The Squire apparently was standing on the hill's summit, very upright and unnaturally tall, his head grotesquely twisted to one side, so that his cheek almost touched his right shoulder. Renfrew shouted, but Hargrave stayed quite still. Then, as the horse mounted the rise on the track, the small hilltop horizon fell . . .

But Hargrave's feet did not fall with it. They were dangling a good two feet from the ground. Renfrew saw the rope then, noosed round his master's neck and tied firmly to the lowest branch of the oak above him. It was quite obvious that Hargrave had been dead for several hours.

Renfrew didn't touch anything. He headed the mare round and urged her back to the farm as fast as she would go.

★ ★ ★

About noon that day the Hargrave Farm received two visitors. Victoria Lincoln drove the car right into the yard this time. Caroline jumped down and went over, reaching for the knocker. Before she touched it the door opened. A thin, tired-looking individual stood there, regarding them dispiritedly. Carol nodded, said; 'Good morning, sir.' Miss Lincoln came up behind her.

'Yes, ladies — what can I do for you?'

Victoria said:

'We'd like to see Mrs. Hargrave, if it's

possible. Is she in?'

'Yes, she's in — but she's not seeing anyone. She's very upset about her husband and she's only just finished being worried sick by the police. Anyhow — what d'you want with her?'

Victoria paused, then showed the man her card.

'Actually, Miss Lawrence, from St. Hilda's, called us in to see if we could discover anything about Mr. Edsel Baxter. This is my assistant, by the way — Miss Caroline Gerrard. And may I ask who you are, sir?'

He grinned, nodding towards Caroline.

'All right — pleased to meet you, ladies. Lionel Baxter's my name — I've a small farm near Shepton Mallet. Mrs. Hargrave is my sister and Edsel my younger brother. She 'phoned me this morning, told me what had happened, asked me to come over and look after things. What is it you want her for? Anything particular?'

'Matter of fact, Mr. Baxter — we suspect foul play. We think your sister may be able to help us . . .'

There was a pause. Mr. Baxter tightened his lips, then stepped aside.

'Come in, ladies. Reckon there's nothing she can tell you that I can't. Come right in . . . '

They sat in the parlour. Baxter unearthed some of the dead man's wine.

'Must say,' he announced, sipping at his drink, 'I never thought Hargrave'd have shame enough to hang himself.'

'Maybe he was fonder of your brother than anyone thought,' suggested Miss Lincoln gravely. 'Look, Mr. Baxter — that's what we want to know, chiefly. How things stood between Hargrave and your brother.'

'I understand. Well, I'll tell you there was no love lost between them! They'd been at college together, certainly, and they stuck together when they left. Then my sister came on the scene. Edsel and she were of an age and my brother had always constituted himself his sister's protector. Hargrave met her at a dance and they both fell in love. A mighty pretty girl she was in those days, happy as the day is long, always laughing and smiling. Anyhow, against Edsel's express wish she married Hargrave. He swept her off her feet, as they say. That's about what happened.'

'Very interesting, Mr. Baxter. Go on.'

'Edsel was a good sport about it, though. He smiled, wished 'em luck, and went abroad for many a long year.

'But things were very different when he returned. He found that Margaret and Hargrave weren't a happy couple. Edsel asked questions here and there, he found out quite a lot. He found out that Hargrave's heart was black as sin, that he'd broken her heart years ago and was slowly breaking her spirit too, and enjoying the doing of it. And if you ask me, Edsel did away with himself because he knew he couldn't do anything for her — his hands were tied and he couldn't bear to see her suffer. That's my opinion.

'As for Hargrave — well, I don't think be killed himself! No, Miss Lincoln — he's not that type. My idea is that someone who had a grudge agen him lay in wait for him in the wood; and as he rode by in the dark — whoosh! They slipped a rope over his head and strung him up to that there tree!'

'It's possible, Mr. Baxter,' Victoria nodded slowly. 'So the position is, that your brother and Hargrave from being boyhood friends, became bitter enemies?'

'Yes, miss. Why, I remember — it was in this very room. One Whit morning, about a year ago. Edsel had only been back a few days, and the four of us had been out riding together. Hargrave and Margaret started arguing and Hargrave was very rude to her.

'My, you should've seen my brother then! He went for Hargrave, knocked him all over the room, left him lying there by the coalscuttle with a black eye. Aye — Hargrave was scared of Edsel after that!'

Victoria Lincoln put down her glass.

'I'm beginning to understand,' she said. 'I can't tell you much now, Mr. Baxter, but I believe, as you do, that Hargrave was murdered! In case there is some kind of a feud affecting your brother, Mr. Hargrave and your sister, I am putting a detective in here as a farmhand to see that Mrs. Hargrave comes to no harm.'

'Margaret?' Baxter was speechless. 'What could happen to my sister?'

'Merely a matter of precaution and only as a temporary expedient while we complete our investigations,' Victoria spoke reassuringly. 'With Edsel having disappeared into thin air and Hargrave obviously having been murdered anything might happen to your sister, although I don't think anything will. Agreed, Mr. Baxter?'

'Anything you say, Miss Lincoln. If you think there is more in this than meets the eye — why, I'm as anxious as you to clear it up.'

He saw them to the door; walked across to the car with them and saluted as Victoria drove away.

★   ★   ★

Carol was very thoughtful on the return journey and suddenly she said:

'Vicky, you are expecting Mrs. Hargrave to go on a journey soon, aren't you?'

'Why Carol, I do believe you are beginning to read my very thoughts. What

125

made you think that?'

'Well, putting in a detective to protect her, for one thing,' replied Carol. 'That was only a subterfuge I'm sure. Don't you think that if I was to disguise myself and watch the station when the trains leave you would be doubly sure of learning all her movements? After all, a handyman on a farm cannot always be watching his mistress!'

Miss Lincoln could not disguise her pleasure at this concrete proof of the excellent way her assistant was adopting her own methods when working on a case. The investigator suddenly decided not to put on another detective to watch the station as she had intended, and instead to let Carol have her chance; for she knew that her assistant had been exceedingly clever at dramatics while at Shelburne.

'A very good idea, Carol,' she said, with a smile. 'And what's more, I'm going to leave the whole of the railway part to you; which means that you must follow Mrs. Hargrave wherever she goes and report to me when she arrives at her destination wherever that may be.'

Carol's eyes were shining with excitement as she almost jumped out of the car.

'I won't let you down, Vicky,' she said. Then realising her little slip she added: 'Sorry, Miss Lincoln, I'm afraid it's always 'Vicky' in my thoughts.'

'Then let it be 'Vicky' whenever we are alone, shall we, Carol?'

'You bet, Vicky!'

* * *

One morning a week later Victoria received a 'phone call from the detective she'd put in at Hargrave Farm. It appeared she had been well advised to have the station watched, for Lionel Baxter apparently had warned his sister she was being watched and she had slipped away while he was otherwise occupied at Baxter's orders. One piece of news interested her especially: a letter had been received the day before addressed to Mrs. Hargrave bearing the postmark 'Marseilles', which, to say the least, caused quite a stir in the household.

Carol not having reported as usual that day, Victoria left a message in the event of her assistant 'phoning, and at once drove to the station where she learned that Mrs. Hargrave had boarded the train for Southampton, and that a rough-looking lad, who was carrying her bag, accidentally had been left on the train when it started.

The investigator then repaired to the local police station where the Inspector was only too willing to assist her by placing the facilities of the law at her disposal.

Various 'phone calls brought to light the fact that an air liner for Marseilles was due to depart from the airport soon after the train from Radstock arrived, which it did while Victoria was 'phoning.

She was just considering her next move when a call came through from Carol who had tailed Mrs. Hargrave to the airport but could not follow her on board as a passport was required and hers was in Victoria's possession. Anyhow, dressed as she was she'd probably have found herself in prison if she had used her own passport.

Miss Lincoln immediately ordered her to resume her own identity and wait at the aerodrome until the detective arrived; which she did some ninety minutes later. Before she left the friendly Inspector, however, she had chartered a special 'plane, also 'phoned the Marseilles *Gendarmerie* and arranged to have Mrs. Hargrave's movements watched.

★　★　★

While they were on their way to Marseilles Victoria complimented Carol on the clever manner in which she had followed her quarry, especially in 'accidentally' being left on the train with Mrs. Hargrave.

'Well,' said Carol, quietly, 'I found it was one thing to act a part on the stage with set phrases to say and things to do, and quite another to be another person and live and act as another person would do. Still the experience will, I know, help me to be more useful to you in future, Vicky.'

'Not a shadow of doubt about that, Carol.'

They were met at the airport by a

gendarme in uniform, who informed them in voluble French which Carol at any rate, followed with difficulty, that Mrs. Hargrave had proceeded straight to the *Hotel Rivoli.*

A taxi, driven in the breakneck manner usual with French drivers, soon brought them to the magnificent portals of the *Hotel Rivoli*, where they were met by a detective in plain clothes, who imparted certain information to Victoria in precise, if a little laboured, English.

'She's in the restaurant now,' he said. 'Monsieur Ercole Barton has just joined her.'

'Who is Ercole Barton?' asked Victoria.

'He is well-known here; a naturalised Englishman, although lately he has been occupied abroad rather a lot.'

'Thanks very much, Monsieur, for all you have done,' said the detective. 'And tell my friends at headquarters that I am only too pleased to reciprocate at any time they require help in England.'

'It is nothing that we have done,' Mademoiselle. The *Gendarmerie* is always at your service!'

Victoria and Carol went to the snack bar at the end of the restaurant and ordered coffees.

'See her, Carol?' the detective asked.

'Yes, Vicky — she's in that left corner, near the window.'

Victoria stared for a long time. Then she said:

'That's Edsel Baxter with her, Carol. Just as I thought. Brother and sister are united again.'

'Mr. Baxter?' Caroline's voice echoed her amazement. 'I never dreamt — '

'Of course you didn't. Nor did anybody else — that was the whole idea! He built up a *false* Baxter, whom he disposed of when the time came; so that he could emerge, as his real self, whom no one knew! Actually, all this began that Whit Monday about a year ago when Hargrave was rude to Margaret in front of Baxter. Remember what Lionel Baxter told us? Well — that was the last straw for Baxter, and he vowed to do something about it.

'Think, my dear! A year ago he was a different man, but after his fight with Hargrave he began to change. A year ago he began to limp. A year ago he began to put on weight, a year ago he began to lose all his money. All for one purpose — to build up a *different* Baxter, one who was anxious to leave this life.

'He padded himself gradually into stoutness; hence his anger at being seen in his night things, without his pads — which also explains why the house-keeper thought he looked thinner. He walked normally in his bedroom each day so that his acquired limp wouldn't get the better of him. He slipped up there all right! He'd never imagine Mrs. Simon would hear him. 'He kept an attaché case in the attic, packed with the few essentials he'd need when he left. This explains that clean patch I told you about.

'Very well. The time arrives — and he goes out one evening and disappears. He shaves, disposes of his limp, his false stoutness — and presto! He sets out an entirely new man! No need for him to hide because nobody recognises him, nobody knows him. Simple — and very clever! Don't you think so?

'Now for Hargrave. Baxter knew his

habits, knew how he rode back in the dark hours of the night from Frome, after market days. So he went to Wyandotte Wood, and waited for his enemy . . .

'Remember that paper we found in his desk? It was a circus handbill, with Baxter's name on it. 'Master of the Rope,' he was billed as. 'Miracle Worker with Lariats, Lassoes and Bolasses'! See? As soon as I heard Hargrave had died by a rope — well, I wondered . . .

'Now suppose, I reasoned, my theory was correct? Baxter and Mrs. Hargrave would soon be meeting each other; so I reckoned if we could watch her, she'd lead us to him, in good time.

'Hence my fairy story to Lionel. I daren't let him think what I suspected or he'd have told her, and furthermore he'd never have agreed to us putting a man in there.'

Caroline nodded slowly. This, she realised with a quick little shudder, was her very first murder case! Miss Lincoln would forgive her if she didn't grasp everything all at once.

They stood looking down the restaurant to where Baxter and Margaret leaned across their table, conversing earnestly.

'I'm beginning to understand, Miss Lincoln. I remember Baxter's photo now! It's the same height, the same head . . . there's no mistaking him!' Her heart began to thump a little. 'What do we do now? Are you going to have him arrested . . . in here?'

Victoria Lincoln sipped her coffee. Her dark eyes were half closed as she gazed at her young assistant.

'I wonder if we have sufficient proof? Even if extradition could be arranged, which I doubt,' she murmured. 'I wonder if we have a shred of *real* evidence? You see, Baxter has everything cut and dried about who he's supposed to be *now*. So how are we going to *prove* anything?'

Surely *someone* will recognize him?' Carol said. 'What about Miss Lawrence — and all the St. Hilda's girls?'

'Ah! Neither Marion nor girls have seen him like he is now! Remember he's only been at St. Hilda's about six months; he went there *after* he began limping, *after* he'd become stout . . . and with his beard. Even Mrs. Simon's never seen him like he is now. I tell you, Carol . . . it's going to be difficult to prove anything.'

Carol waited a moment. Then:

'What's our next move, Vicky?'

'Well, I'll make my report to Miss Lawrence, and to the police. I only hope they don't laugh at me and say I'm suffering from delusions! Look, dear . . . will you slip and get Miss Lawrence on the 'phone? Here's her number — it doesn't take long to get a trunk call to England from here!'

When Carol had gone Victoria Lincoln turned, leaned against the snack bar, looked down the restaurant.

She was quietly pensive, for she was finding it in her heart to be sympathetic towards the murderer of Hargrave. Nevertheless, human life is sacred and there was a penalty for taking it . . .

Wherever her sympathy might lie she had her duty to do.

5

The Visitors Who Vanished

Victoria Lincoln, private detective, showed her assistant, Caroline Gerrard, the card that had been enclosed in a letter she'd received by that morning's post.

'Something rather exciting may come of this, Carol! It's from Mr. Graham West, the well-known art dealer.'

Caroline fixed hero-worshipping blue eyes on her brilliant employer. 'Great! That's just what I'm longing for — plenty of excitement! What sort of trouble is Mr. West in?'

'He's in a nasty mix-up, by the sound of this,' Victoria smiled as she waved Mr. West's letter. 'Someone who was supposed to be Professor Garston, the famous sculptor, called on him one evening; and later vanished into thin air from Mr. West's study — taking with him a valuable solid silver statuette of a crusading knight on horseback. The police were called immediately; but they've been unable to discover what happened either to the bogus Professor or the statuette.'

'That's a funny how-de-do, isn't it?' Caroline murmured. 'Surely someone must have seen the thief leave? Surely — '

'Not according to Mr. West's statement,' Miss Lincoln broke in. 'The visitor, it seems, was left alone for less than two minutes; and in that time the ground fairly opened and swallowed him. The whole thing is — '

She paused as the buzzer in the outer office sounded. Next moment her secretary tapped on the door and opened it.

'A Mr. Graham West is here, Miss Lincoln.'

'All right, Miss Wentworth. I'll see him right away.'

Graham West was tall and thin, with restless dark eyes and slender hands that fidgeted nervously. Victoria placed a chair for him on the opposite side of her desk, while Caroline sat at her smaller one near the window.

Miss Lincoln said:

'Perhaps you'll tell me your story right from the beginning, Mr. West. It sounds a most extraordinary affair, from your letter.'

Mr. West placed his hat and gloves on the desk. He indicated Caroline with a slight movement of his head.

'Who is this young lady?'

'My assistant, Miss Gerrard,' Victoria said gravely.

'I see. Well, Miss Lincoln, I'll be more than glad to give this baffling mystery into your capable hands. The police have been working on it for a fortnight but they're getting absolutely nowhere. Let's hope your more — er, unorthodox methods will show quicker results!'

'We can only hope!' murmured Victoria Lincoln. 'And now, Mr. West, if you'll begin . . . '

'Ah, yes.' Graham West leaned back, crossed his legs, placed the tips of his fingers together, tapping them nervously. 'It all began the day I inserted an advertisement in the *Kent Messenger*, about some antiques I had for sale at my home — Grayson Manor, near Maidstone. The next morning I had a 'phone call from someone who said he was Professor Garston. I'd never seen Garston, but I'd heard of his work. He wanted to know if I had anything in statuettes, and I said 'Yes'. Would it be convenient, he asked, if he came down that evening about seven?

'I told him I'd be pleased to receive him. Now at the Manor, I keep my collection in my study on the first floor. There are some priceless pieces in there, Miss Lincoln, and I never leave the door unlocked. I have the only key; and even when the maid is in there to clean, I'm there, too, and I wait until she's finished. I want to emphasise this point very strongly. No one is ever allowed in that room unless I'm there too. So you can understand that no one else possibly could have stolen that statuette save this bogus Professor.

'Anyway, at seven that evening, there I was in my study, waiting. At a few minutes past there's a knock on the door. Parker, my butler, says, 'Professor Garston to see you, sir.' Then the door opens and in walks the Professor. He has a black cloak and cane, a dark Vandyke beard, flowing moustache and a mop of fuzzy hair. At the time I thought vaguely that he seemed to be all hair!

'Anyway, we had a chat and he examined my collection, picking out a few pieces he was interested in.' Mr. West raised his hand, stabbed the air with his forefinger in dramatic fashion. 'Now listen carefully to this, ladies . . . here is where the funny business starts . . .

'Suddenly the Professor sat down, clutching at his heart. 'Excuse me, Mr. West,' he gasps, 'It's my heart; could you get me a drink of water, please?'

'The bathroom was just outside my door — about ten yards down the landing. I dashed out, filled a tumbler with water, and dashed back. The Professor had vanished! Absolutely vanished into thin air!' Mr. West leaned forward, smacked the desk top with his fist. 'There wasn't a trace of him anywhere in the house or grounds; and when I checked my collection I found a very valuable silver statuette of a horseman was missing. What d'you make of it, Miss Lincoln?'

Victoria's face was grave as she made a

few notes on a pad.

'First, Mr. West — are there any other exits from your study save through the door?'

'None. The windows are leaded, and they open only at the top. About six inches, that's all, for ventilation. They're set high in the wall too — and there's a drop of about fifty feet outside. It's altogether impossible for anyone to get out that way.'

'All right. Was there anyone about — I mean, near the study — when you dashed back with the water and found your visitor gone?'

Graham West scratched his chin. His brows were drawn in thought.

'Let's see . . . yes . . . there was young Lawrence Bentley in his bedroom just down the landing — he heard me shout, and ran out. And Parker, the butler, was in the hall, just beginning his rounds of drawing the curtains. Then as I dashed downstairs the front door opened and Randolf Bentley came in.'

'That's very interesting,' Victoria murmured. 'There we have three people who *should* have seen the Professor making his getaway. And none of them could help you?'

'They could not,' Mr. West's voice was grim. 'They were as completely mystified as I was.'

Vicky was thoughtful for some moments as she made mental notes.

'The Bentleys, Mr. West ... you mention Lawrence and Randolf. Friends, I take it? On a visit to you?'

'Exactly. Lawrence is on vacation from the university. His father is an old friend. Actually Randolf is an art dealer, too. I suppose you could call us rivals, in a way.' West shifted uncomfortably in his seat. 'I'm bound to tell you this, Miss Lincoln, though it goes against the grain. Randolf Bentley has been anxious to buy certain of my statuettes for some time past. You see, there's three that I vowed never to sell ... the silver horseman, another in bronze of a Greek god holding a sword, and a third — a smaller cup in solid gold of a water nymph about to dive. 'Those are the ones Randolf has pestered me to sell him — and it's the silver one that's missing!'

At her desk Caroline Gerrard was tense with excitement. Graham West had brought them a mystery that promised to be very intriguing . . .

Miss Lincoln nodded slowly.

'Very interesting indeed, Mr. West. Any particular reason why you won't part with them?'

'Well, they were handed down to me by my father — and he'd always been very fond of them. Now here's another point Miss Lincoln: that silver horseman statuette is on an ebony base — and it has a false bottom. Inside, I'd hidden a necklace worth many thousands of pounds!'

'Good heavens!' Victoria was genuinely alarmed. 'Don't tell me the thief had that, too?'

She breathed relief when West smiled, shook his head.

'Thank goodness, no. The very morning of the day when the Professor came, I took out the necklace to examine it and for no good reason at all, I didn't put it back in the horseman, but in the bronze statuette — for each of the three has an ebony stand which is hollow inside. Don't ask me why I did this — I don't know! Fate must have guided me, I suppose.'

'It's truly amazing, I grant you,' said Miss Lincoln. 'Forgive me if I say it seems rather silly to keep such a valuable thing in a statuette. What's wrong with your safe?'

Graham West shrugged.

'I suppose I'm eccentric, Miss Lincoln. For one thing, my safe's in the library, which can be entered through the window; and for another, the safe is always the first thing in a house that thieves make for. No — it's always appealed to me as the very safest place to hide the necklace . . . in one of the statuettes.'

'Well, it looks as if the thief found out about it, doesn't it?' Victoria Lincoln asked. 'Obviously, the whole thing was staged with that one express purpose — to get hold of the statuette containing the necklace. The thief shammed sickness just to get you out of the room for a moment . . . time enough for him to grab the statuette and stage his disappearing act. I suppose, when you fetched the police, they immediately contacted Professor Garston's home?'

'Naturally. But he was away on a lecture in Scotland. There's no possible chance of him being involved.'

'H'm'm. Now — who else knew about the necklace being hidden in the statuette?'

'No one — absolutely no one.' Mr. West was emphatic. 'I'd never breathed it to a soul — not even to my wife.'

'I see. Well . . . have you any theories . . . any idea at all who it could be?'

'My dear young lady, I haven't! All I can say is . . . well, Randolf Bentley had wanted those statuettes badly for a long time, and both he and his son were more or less on the spot when the theft was committed. Here's a point: Lawrence is rather keen on magic. He's always doing conjuring tricks, playing practical jokes and such-like.'

Victoria nodded.

'So you think he might have been persuaded by his father to dress up in that cloak and beard, etcetera, and steal a statuette . . . that it was just by chance he grabbed the silver horseman?'

145

Graham West shrugged.

'I hardly like to suggest it, Miss Lincoln, but in such an extraordinary case — well, one is forced to advance some idea . . . '

'Quite.' Miss Lincoln rose, signed to Caroline. 'Very well, Mr. West . . . just what d'you want us to do?'

'Come down to the Manor as my guests!' Mr. West spoke eagerly. 'Mingle with the household — I'm certain your clever brains will unearth something. I wish I could give you more to work on, but I can't. It's up to you now, ladies!'

Victoria Lincoln walked to the door, opened it.

'We'll be on our way within the hour, Mr. West.'

The art dealer shook hands with the detective and her assistant and bowed himself out.

Miss Lincoln took her hat from the stand, walked to the mirror. Caroline thought she looked very lovely, in her smartly-tailored black velour two-piece and primrose silk scarf. Softly Victoria patted her dark waves beneath the wide velvet hat, which matched her costume.

''Phone up for the car, Carol, there's a dear,' she murmured.

Caroline's spirits bubbled gleefully as she reached for the 'phone. With Victoria Lincoln on the job, how could they fail . . . ?

★　★　★

Dusk was falling as Victoria turned the car into the long winding drive of Grayson Manor. Lights winked cheerily from a dozen or more windows as they pulled up before the beautiful old house.

At supper Graham West introduced them as his friends, making no mention that they were there on business. Obeying her employer's instructions, Caroline watched the other guests carefully — most especially, Randolf Bentley and his son, Lawrence.

Randolf was big and hearty. The hard muscles of his shoulders fairly made his chair creak when he leaned back, as he often did, to give a hearty laugh. Carol couldn't imagine him stooping to anything underhand; Lawrence she wasn't so sure about, though. He was pale, dark, a little weak and sickly looking. Graham West's daughter, Sylvia, sat on Carol's right — a cheery, freckled-faced youngster with a mop of carroty hair. Caroline didn't waste time during the meal. Cleverly, persistently, she questioned Sylvia.

'What d'you think of Lawrence, Sylvia?'

'Him? Oh, not so much!' Sylvia grinned. 'Trouble is, Carol, he seems to have taken quite a fancy to me! Done nothing but pester me to go out with him ever since he's been here. I don't like his style and I keep saying 'No'. One night about a week ago he became angry. Honestly — you'd have laughed your eyes out. We were in the drawing room and he begged me to go to a dance in the town. He was really wild when I refused, started being quite objectionable. Dad came in and heard him — told him if he didn't behave himself and stop bothering me he'd have to leave. He and Dad have been daggers drawn since then.'

'H'm'm . . . they say he's a bit of a japer?'

'Yes — he's not bad at conjuring, and he knows a few good card tricks.'

'D'you think he had anything to do with that business of the disappearing Professor?'

Sylvia chuckled. 'What, Lawrence? Never in the world! I don't think he's enough sand to pull off a thing like that!'

Later, in their own room, Caroline told her boss of this conversation.

'I was just thinking, Miss Lincoln — supposing Lawrence did it out of revenge — to get his own back for the chalking off Mr. West gave him over Sylvia?'

The detective pursed her lips.

'Well — it's an idea, Carol. My own questioning has established that the thief didn't fly down the stairs and get away through the front door — which was his only line of escape. For Parker would have seen him ... and he'd have practically collided with Mr. Bentley, who was coming in at that moment, as Mr. West told us. It just seems that the study floor opened and swallowed him.'

She glanced at her watch.

'Nine o'clock, Carol. Mr. West will be in his study now. I said we'd go and take a look round. Come on.'

They went down to the first floor. The study, they found, was a small room, tastefully furnished, with shuttered windows and cream-distempered walls. A cheery fire burnt brightly in the grate.

Mr. West watched the detective as she examined the walls.

'Are they quite solid, Mr. West?' Victoria asked.

'Absolutely! Solid brick, Miss Lincoln. It's a modern room, this one . . . I had it built on when I took over the place. Have a good look round. Try it for yourself.'

'I will. Carol, will you go over every inch of the floor, dear? I'll do the same with the walls.'

After twenty minutes' painstaking searching and rapping they were convinced there was no hidden exit from the room. They stayed chatting awhile with Mr. West. Victoria asked about the servants.

'There's only two — and a maid,' replied Mr. West. 'Parker and his wife have been with me for years — and Ellen came from a friend of mine, she's very highly recommended. I don't think we'll find a solution in that direction, Miss Lincoln!'

'Mr. West,' Victoria said after a pause, 'take your mind back to the night of the theft. Think very, very carefully. Was there anything — did anything strike you as being the least suspicious, the least out of the ordinary?' In slow, measured tones she repeated the question. 'Think, Mr. West, as if your very life was depending on it! Surely there must be *something* . . . if there is, tell me . . . no matter how trivial you think it is . . . '

Graham West paced up and down, his head lowered, his brows drawn deep in thought. Finally he halted before the detective and her assistant. He laughed nervously.

'You'll probably think me crazy, Miss Lincoln — but when I ran out of here, after I'd come back with the water — I noticed that the curtains of the landing window opposite were drawn . . . and they hadn't been when I'd run out to fetch the water! Here . . . I'll show you.'

He went to the door, opened it, beckoned them through. Opposite they saw a high window covered by heavy blue brocade curtains.

'See? That's the one I mean. I noticed it particularly because it wasn't really dark — it was only just beginning to get dusk. I thought nothing of it at the time, and I haven't done so since. I only mention it now because you ask me if I — '

'Quite.' Miss Lincoln nodded. 'It's these little points that count just the same.'

She went across the landing, pulled aside the curtains. Behind them was a broad window ledge on which reposed a carved copper flowerpot containing a single flowering geranium.

They said goodnight to Mr. West, went back to their rooms. Victoria sat on the bed, swinging her shapely silk-clad legs.

'The clue of the drawn curtains!' she murmured, with a smile and a wink at Caroline. 'And what a clue! Are we to believe Mr. West?'

'No — hardly. That means someone drew them between him leaving the study for the water and returning with it. Someone drew them — but why? And who?'

'Didn't he say that Parker was in the hall when he raced down — just beginning the rounds of drawing the curtains?'

'He did, Carol. I remember. Well, we haven't spoken to Parker yet. Shall we slip down and do it now?'

They found the manservant in the kitchen, taking his ease with a bottle of ale and the evening paper. He was a tall, dignified, white-haired retainer of the old school, with inscrutable eyes that were a little too frosty for Carol's liking. He scratched his head when Miss Lincoln questioned him about the curtains.

'Well, ma'am, I really can't remember . . . it's been nearly a fortnight ago, mind. If they *were* drawn when I came up to them, well — I wouldn't think a deal about it.'

'And while you were in the hall that night you're absolutely certain no one ran through to the front door?'

'I'll swear they didn't, ma'am. Why Mr. Bentley came in as the master was running downstairs. He'd have seen, if anyone did. You ask Mr. Bentley, ma'am.'

They went slowly back upstairs. On the first floor landing Victoria paused, gripped her assistant's arm. From below came the tinkling notes of a piano. Carol said:

'What now, Miss Lincoln? That'll be Sylvia, I expect — she's studying the piano, she told me; and no doubt little Lawrence will be turning the music for her.'

Victoria nodded.

'That's just what I thought, Carol.' She pulled her young assistant past the study door, down the landing till they stood outside Lawrence Bentley's room. 'Go to the top of the stairs and stay on guard, my dear. If Lawrence comes in sight, give a little whistle. I'm going to search his room!'

Caroline sped away on her errand, her heart pounding with excitement. From the tense, eager look in Miss Lincoln's eyes she knew her employer was on the track of something. She leaned against the balustrade at the stair-head, looked down into the hall . . .

Meanwhile, Victoria Lincoln softly turned the knob of Lawrence Bentley's door, and crept in. It was a small room, with a three-quarter bed, dressing chest, and wardrobe. Quickly Victoria pulled out the dresser drawers. Nothing there save ordinary articles of clothing . . .

Two suits hung in the wardrobe; at the bottom, another drawer ran its entire length. Victoria bent, pulled at the handles. Obviously it wasn't used very much, for it stuck badly. Finally, however, it came open; and as the detective peered inside she gave a low whistle of amazement.

She reached inside, pulled out a long black cloak that lay bundled up in a corner. As she unrolled it, there fell out a portion of darkish hair shaped like a beard, and a full wig of grey hair!

At the back of the drawer was a black, silver-knobbed cane . . .

'What d'you think of it, Caroline?'

The detective and her assistant sat in

their room discussing Victoria's extraordinary discovery.

'Why, doesn't it point to Lawrence Bentley being the guilty party?' asked Carol. 'Surely you've enough evidence now to have him arrested?'

Miss Lincoln wasn't convinced though.

'I'm going to sleep on it first, Carol. Maybe I'll have decided by morning.'

They both retired to their beds. An hour later Victoria was still tossing and turning, unable to dismiss the fascinating mystery of the disappearing Professor from her mind. Time passed. Gradually silence shut down over the house as one by one the various members drifted off to bed.

Midnight tolled from a nearby church tower. Half past . . . Victoria rose, went to get a glass of water. She had just taken a sip, when a peculiar sound caught her attention, Setting down the glass she crossed quickly to the door. She opened it softly, stood listening intently. From below came the muffled sound of someone singing!

Miss Lincoln crept out, down the

landing to the first floor. The sounds came from Graham West's study. She was about to move towards it when a tall figure crossed the hall and began to mount the stairs. Victoria crouched back into the shadows round the corner of the wall. It was Parker, the venerable butler . . .

Keenly the detective watched as Parker went to the study door and knocked. A thick voice bade him enter.

Victoria Lincoln decided to take a chance. As Parker opened the door she crept forward, keeping close to the wall. She heard Mr. West say: 'Bring me another bottle of wine, Parker. At once! D'you hear?'

She caught in her breath sharply. Graham West was the worse for drink! She could tell that by his loud, uneven voice, by the way he grunted between each word.

Then Parker said:

'Sir, it's nearly one o'clock. Don't you think you'd better retire now? Everyone in the house is asleep, if you'll pardon me, sir.'

There was a pause, then West growled: 'Oh, all right . . . I didn't realise it was so late. All right, Parker, you can go to bed.'

'Yes, sir. Thank you, sir.'

Every nerve tingling with excitement, Miss Lincoln raced back to her room: This little incident had given her an idea that might lead to a solution of the baffling mystery surrounding Grayson Manor . . .

Snug between the sheets again, she felt the thrill of the hunter at the first sight of the quarry.

★　★　★

At breakfast next morning while Parker and Ellen were busily serving, Victoria surprised everyone by suddenly announcing:

'I think you were very wise, Mr. West, to transfer that necklace to the bronze statuette!'

Beyond Miss Lincoln, only Caroline and West himself knew what lay behind this startling remark. Randolf Bentley and Mrs. West spoke together.

'What's this, Graham?'

'Hiding necklaces, old man? Scared of robbers?'

Laughingly, West explained. Slowly the meal progressed. One by one the guests finished and departed, till only Mr. and Mrs. West, Victoria and Carol remained. Graham West was lighting a cigarette when the 'phone shrilled.

He went to the sideboard. Miss Lincoln and her assistant exchanged significant glances as he lifted the receiver.

'Mr. West here . . . yes . . . who? Lewis Carway . . . Bond Street . . . ah, yes, Mr. Carway . . .

'Certainly I'll be in this evening. I'll be glad to show you my collection . . . I'll expect you about seven . . . yes . . . good-bye . . . '

'Another customer, Graham?' Mrs. West asked primly.

'Yes, my dear. Well-known collector from Bond Street. I've passed his shop many times. I think I may do some good business with him.'

They excused themselves, left the room. Victoria and Caroline went for a stroll in the grounds. Carol said eagerly:

'Miss Lincoln, it looks as though our scheme will be successful! D'you think Mr. Carway will be the thief again, in disguise?'

'That's what we hope to find out, Carol. Now tonight at seven, you park yourself on the landing just across from West's study — you can hide just inside the bathroom, eh? And I'll be in the hall . . . so if there's any funny business, between us, we ought to discover something!'

So at ten to seven that evening the detective and her assistant left their room to take up their posts. But as they crossed to the stairs they heard Parker's deep voice saying from the floor below:

'This way, Mr. Carway. Mr. West is in his study. He's expecting you.'

Victoria caught Caroline's arm.

'Come on, Carol. I want to get a look at this Mr. Carway. He *would* be early!'

The flight of stairs leading to the first floor was long and winding. They were a little breathless when they reached the landing — only to find the immaculate

Parker coming out and closing the study door.

He bowed politely as he passed them. Disconsolately they watched his broad back proceed serenely down to the hall.

Victoria spoke softly.

'All right, Carol . . . On your way. Don't take your eyes off the study door — and when they come out, get a good look at Carway. They oughtn't to be long.'

Carol nodded, crept over to the bathroom, stood just inside the door. Miss Lincoln went downstairs.

Caroline waited, her heart thumping with excitement. Five minutes passed . . . ten . . . twenty. Her eyes glued to the study door, she shifted from one foot to the other. No sound whatever came from behind the study door. She began to get uneasy. Surely two art dealers doing business should make some noise?

Carol waited the full half-hour, then crept out to the head of the stairs. She whistled softly. Miss Lincoln appeared from the shadows near the front door and came up at once.

'Carol — what is it?'

'I think something's wrong, Miss Lincoln! There's absolutely no sound from the study. I'm sure something's happened to Mr. West!'

'All right — we'll see.'

They ran back to the study. Victoria bent, listening intently. Silence, as of the grave. Slowly she reached for the doorknob, turned it, flung the door open.

In the room the lights blazed, the fire crackled. They crowded in, looking round eagerly. At first they didn't see Mr. West. Then Carol gave a startled gasp, pointing to a high-backed chair beyond the fireplace.

They dashed over. Victoria's face was pale and grim as she bent to examine their unconscious host. He lay behind the chair, his legs drawn up queerly, his face dead white save for a trickle of blood across his cheek from a wound on his forehead.

Caroline gazed round the room in utter bewilderment. She found it impossible to believe her own eyes.

For of Mr. West's visitor, the mysterious Lewis Carway, there was not the slightest trace or sign . . .

When Mr. West had been revived and his wound dressed, Victoria Lincoln asked about Lewis Carway. But Graham West shook his head vaguely.

'I never saw him, Miss Lincoln! I heard Parker announce him — I was busy sorting over some books and had my back to the door. I was just about to turn when something hit me on the head and everything went black.'

Parker himself couldn't help very much either.

'He was nothing to look at, ma'am,' he said, in answer to Victoria's question. 'A smallish man, dark with a big black hat. He must have hit the master and then run downstairs and out through the front door.'

Victoria said nothing. Mr. West was carefully checking over his collection, to make sure nothing was missing. Next moment he gave a startled yell.

'The bronze statuette!' he gasped. 'The Greek god . . . it's missing!'

This was amazing news indeed. Presently Victoria drew her host discreetly aside.

'Tell everyone to clear out, Mr. West. I've a little plan I want to put to you that I think will trap the thief.'

When they were alone, she and Carol talked with him long and earnestly. Later that evening, around midnight, sounds of raucous singing could be heard coming from the study. This time, Miss Lincoln summoned Parker, also Lawrence and Randolf Bentley.

'I'm afraid Mr. West has taken a little too much wine, gentlemen. Miss Gerrard and I are quite unable to sleep for the noise. I suggest we get him gently to bed.'

They went into the study. Mr. West was seated near the fire, a bottle of wine at his elbow.

When he saw his visitors he began to mumble thickly.

'Ah, don't want to go to sleep! Had a drop too much to drink — always see ghosts when I've had too much wine. Saw one last time — ugh! Kept wanting me to say where I'd hidden my necklace. Yesh . . . and I was just going to tell him, too — but I woke up! Listen, folks — don't put me to bed . . . don't want ghosts to come . . .'

After a deal of gentle persuasion however, they managed to get him upstairs. Victoria went back to her room, where Carol awaited her eagerly expectant.

'It's working beautifully, my dear!' Miss Lincoln's eyes shone excitedly. 'All we have to do now is wait for the grand finale!'

They waited until everything was quiet, then they crept downstairs and into Graham West's bedroom. They crouched in the shadows on each side of the door. From the bed came their host's heavy, regular breathing.

Nearly an hour went by as they crouched there, scarcely daring to breathe. Then the door opened softly and a white, ghostly figure stole in. Carol could hardly repress a scream. It glided to the bed, bent over Mr. West and prodded him. Then it began to speak in deep, sepulchral tones.

'Graham West . . . I am the ghost of your grandfather . . . I command you to say where you have hidden the pearl necklace! Do you hear? I command you to speak the truth!'

Miss Lincoln's hand reached for the switch. As the room flooded with light she said sharply:

'There you are, men . . . get him! Don't let him get away . . . '

Two burly men sprang from behind a wardrobe placed across one corner. Before the 'ghost' could realise what was happening, they'd snatched off the sheet that covered him from head to foot. As the handcuffs clicked on his wrists Caroline echoed Victoria Lincoln's amazed exclamation.

For there, scowling darkly round the room stood Parker, the dignified butler!

'Drastic measures for a drastic case, gentlemen!' Miss Lincoln explained later to an admiring group. 'The mystery of the disappearing art dealers was just a little too baffling to be genuine. People simply don't vanish into thin air, as Garston and Carway apparently did.

'I imagine all this began when Mr. West, one evening when he'd taken a little too much wine, confided to Parker about the necklace being hidden in the silver statuette. Parker, who'd been hard pressed for money for some time, determined to get it. But how could he get into the study? Mr. West always kept it locked, and kept the only key on his person.

'Parker noticed his employer's advert, and his crafty brain evolved the idea of impersonating Professor Garston. He 'phoned Mr. West, fixed the fake appointment. Then from a theatrical shop in Maidstone he bought beard, wig, cloak, etcetera, dressed himself up, watched his chance and walked boldly up to the study, announcing himself as he opened the door!

'Then he staged the fainting fit. While Mr. West fetched the water he snatched off his disguise, grabbed the statuette, and dashed from the room, throwing his beard, wig and so on, on the window ledge opposite and drawing the curtains. Then, when Mr. West came running downstairs; he was calmly going about his duties in the hall! Later, to throw suspicion on someone else, he collected his traps from the window ledge and hid them in Lawrence Bentley's wardrobe; no doubt intending to 'discover' them by accident a few days later and report the matter to his employer.

'When Parker examined his spoils he received his first set-back. For that very morning Mr. West's subconscious mind had, very fortunately: been at work. He must have realised he'd told someone about that necklace whilst he'd been drinking the night before. So he changed the necklace over from the silver statuette to the bronze one. Imagine Parker's chagrin when he discovered all his clever scheming had been in vain!

'When I found the disguise in Lawrence Bentley's wardrobe I did a little reconstruction. At that time, I admit, I actually suspected Lawrence. So I laid my plans with Mr. West — for it was essential that the crook be tempted to make another attempt, if we were to catch him.

'So at breakfast I made it plain to one and all that the necklace was hidden in the bronze statuette. Actually, Mr. West had removed it that morning, on my instructions, and placed it in his safe.

'I think you'll agree Parker had plenty of nerve! He actually repeated the scheme he'd attempted with the name of Professor Garston, but this time he didn't risk a long chat with Mr. West. Maybe his 'Lewis Carway' disguise wasn't so good. He was a little early for his appointment, otherwise Miss Gerrard and I would have caught him in the act! We did actually see him coming from the study after he'd struck Mr. West and snatched up the bronze statuette.

'Anyway, this attempt failed also. He'd secured two statuettes now — but still no necklace. So I persuaded Mr. West to stage his little drunken scene, making sure that everyone in the house who could possibly be under suspicion was there to hear him. I felt reasonably sure it would lure the thief to make his third attempt — and I had two detectives from Maidstone, in hiding in Mr. West's room, ready to grab the crook should he come masquerading as a ghost!'

Amid a hushed, almost reverent silence, Victoria Lincoln selected a chocolate from a nearby sweet dish and smiled serenely at the circle of openly admiring faces. Caroline caught her eye and winked . . .

6

From Beyond the Grave

To Victoria Lincoln's suite of offices on the first floor of Kingward House, Regent Street, London, there came, on a crisp morning early in the year, the dignified person of Miss Mary Reid.

She had an appointment, it seemed; for Pamela Wentworth, Victoria's secretary, immediately showed her into the detective's private sanctum, where she and Caroline Gerrard, sat waiting at their respective desks. Miss Reid — tall, aloof, with thin little lips that opened and closed with tight correctness — came straight to the point.

'Miss Lincoln, I've come to you because the police cannot help me. I have nothing to go on except my suspicions, and the law will not act unless you can supply it with facts. But — as my suspicions will not allow me to rest — I'll give you the particulars of my case; with the earnest request that you do your utmost to save my dear sister from a most horrible fate.'

Victoria Lincoln murmured:

'You can rely on our very best efforts, Miss Reid.' She glanced across at her young assistant. 'Carol, dear, will you take a few notes?'

Caroline nodded, blue eyes agleam. She held up her pencil.

'All set, Miss Lincoln!'

Miss Reid went on:

'It all began about three months ago when Lady Enid Carson disappeared. She fell overboard from a Channel steamer, crossing from Dover to Calais. At least, that's the story put out by her husband, Sir Robert Carson. There was a very heavy sea running, he says; and against his wish, Enid left their cabin to go for a stroll on deck. An hour later, she hadn't returned — and no trace of her has been found since.'

Victoria Lincoln looked puzzled.

'You're asking us to believe that Sir Robert killed her ... ? On a small

Channel steamer, crowded with passengers . . . and then threw her body overboard? I'd say, from my own experience of Channel steamers, that it'd be an impossibility, Miss Reid! Someone would have seen him . . . '

'Ah, just one moment!' interrupted Miss Reid. 'It is my firm belief that the unfortunate lady never set foot on that boat at all! For there is not one shred of real evidence to prove that she did so. I've talked to the captain, to the stewardess, to the purser — and not one of them can swear they actually saw her. Officially, of course, she was on board — for Sir Robert had surrendered her ticket to the collector and had received her landing voucher. Nevertheless, I've been unable to find anyone who could say definitely that Sir Robert had his wife with him on that trip.'

She said the last dozen words slowly and with emphasis, leaning forward and tapping the desk top with her finger tips.

'I take it that Enid Carson is a — er, a friend, or a relative, Miss Reid?'

'No. I've never set eyes on the poor

woman; but — Sir Robert Carson has recently become engaged to my dear sister Margaret ... and Margaret had over ten thousand pounds left to her by an uncle about a year ago, Miss Lincoln!'

Victoria nodded. She spoke softly.

'I see. You fear that Carson is marrying your sister for her money — and that when the time is ripe he'll do away with her, too?'

'Exactly! In some way, the scheming scoundrel must be stopped. I dare not think of what might happen to poor Margaret if she marries him!'

'Surely you're not basing your suspicions merely on the fact that three members of the ship's crew can't remember seeing Lady Enid on board that Channel steamer? After all, they wouldn't know her by name. To them, she'd be merely another passenger, wouldn't she?'

'I suppose so; still even the porter can't recollect actually seeing her. He says he remembers Sir Robert because he gave him a large tip — and he also remembers putting Lady Enid's baggage in their cabin, for there were three hat-boxes amongst it and one loose hat.'

'Here's another point.' Caroline watched, engrossed, as Miss Reid's pale brown eyes narrowed and her lips pursed grimly. 'I had occasion to advertise for a new chauffeur about a month ago — and one of the applicants was a William Gaynor, who's been chauffeur to Sir Robert for the past three years. He'd been sacked for no apparent reason, his references were excellent — so I gave him the job. And he's told me some very interesting facts about Sir Robert — and especially about the night he and Lady Enid left their home, Fellsgarth Manor, in Ashford, to drive down to Dover to catch the boat to Calais.'

Both Victoria and Carol felt their interest growing.

'Now the boat left at eleven, prompt,' Mary Reid went on, 'and Gaynor says on that evening about five o'clock, Sir Robert sent for him and said: 'I shan't be wanting you tonight, Gaynor. Lady Enid and I are going to Dover and I'm driving myself. I'll leave the car in the City

Garage, at Dover. You go down by train in the morning and drive it back'.

'Now Gaynor was very surprised at this — for two reasons. He knew that Sir Robert hated driving at night, and more especially did he hate driving in the rain; and Gaynor says that it had simply poured down all that afternoon and that it showed no signs of stopping. In fact, it was still teeming down when, about seven o'clock, Sir Robert and Lady Enid set off.'

Victoria Lincoln nodded slowly. She was beginning now to get the hang of things.

'So you think she was murdered at some point en route — and her body thrown from the car?'

'I do. And by hook or by crook I want you to find the body prove that Sir Robert killed her, and have him arrested!'

'A tall order indeed, madam!' Victoria jumped up, held out her hand, which Miss Reid shook rather timidly. 'We'll take on the case though, and you can rest assured we'll do our utmost to set your mind at ease, one way or the other. I agree there are certain points about the affair which are — to say the least — suspicious.'

When the good lady had gone, Miss Lincoln told her young assistant to ring for the car.

'Fellsgarth Manor is our first port of call, Carol! When we've had a chat with Sir Robert we'll know better how to proceed!'

Caroline nodded. She felt the now familiar thrill tingling her nerves as she reached for the 'phone.

* * *

Towards noon Victoria Lincoln guided her saloon through the lodge gates of Fellsgarth Manor, not far from the pleasant little town of Ashford, in Kent. Carol sat by her side, looking out appreciatively as they glided up a long and winding avenue of poplars, and presently came within sight of the grey manor house.

As they stopped and alighted, a young woman rose from a rustic seat near the porch and came towards them. She was pretty in a rather colourless way; her complexion and features were good but she lacked sparkle. Victoria recognised the type as one simple and weak enough to submit to any personality strong enough to dominate it.

'I'm Miss Margaret Reid,' she began. 'You wish to see Sir Robert, I suppose? Er — is he expecting you?'

Miss Lincoln had her story ready.

'No . . . we're making enquiries on behalf of an insurance company. It's rather urgent.'

'I see. Well — will you go into the hall and ring? One of the maids will take you to his study.'

As they were shown into the study Sir Robert rose from behind his desk and eyed them suspiciously. Victoria smiled her sweetest smile.

'Please sit down, sir. My assistant and I — that is, our people, the North and South Insurance Company, have received an anonymous letter saying that some of your late wife's jewellery has been offered for sale in certain shops in Paris. Now, as we hold a policy on a number of her trinkets, we — '

Her keen eyes never left the baronet's face. She saw a dull flush suddenly stain his heavy cheeks.

Sir Robert's burly figure fairly quivered as he banged the desk, his nostrils twitching.

'By gad, ma'am!' he roared. 'I'd like to get my hands on the scoundrel who wrote such a foul lie! I can account for every one of Enid's jewels. I brought her case back, unopened, after that awful night.

'You have it here now?' asked Victoria softly.

'Eh? No . . . I well, my bank is holding it as security for a small loan. I — '

Sir Robert stopped abruptly. His fierce eyes flashed.

'Look here, I don't like your attitude! Why should I be telling you all this? Why — '

Miss Lincoln held up her hand. Carol marvelled afresh at Victoria's cool confidence.

'It's quite all right, sir — please don't worry about it. Now we know the jewels are safe, well . . . our duty is done. Allow me to offer my sincere sympathy in your very sad bereavement.'

'It was a terrible business,' Sir Robert

said, staring at his desk. 'Enid was such a good sailor, too. Fancy a thing like that happening to her! Although — it was a very wild night, you understand . . . I imagine all the passengers were in their cabins. Even *I* had no desire to venture on deck: but not so my dear wife! I told her not to be so foolish — but she would insist on taking her exercise.' He rose abruptly, his head still lowered. 'She left our cabin — never to return! It was horrible . . . horrible . . . '

He went to the door, held it open. He made it quite obvious that he wished to be alone.

As they drove slowly down the drive Victoria Lincoln said:

'I don't like him, Carol. He's domineering, bad-tempered — and he's short of money. See how that bit slipped out about the bank lending him cash?'

Caroline nodded

'And I bet poor Margaret Reid is completely under his thumb!'

Instead of following the main road back to Ashford, Miss Lincoln turned down a smaller, winding one that apparently bordered the baronet's estate.

'Now we're here we may as well have a good look round!' she said with a smile.

They drove slowly along the narrow lane. On their left, a high lichen-covered wall flanked the manor grounds; on their right, and away to the southeast they could see across the sunlit meadows, the gently rising lines of the Sussex Downs. The scene was one of peace and serenity. It was hard to believe that murder could lurk anywhere near such an enchanted spot . . .

For nearly half a mile they rode thus. Then, at a corner where the lane forked, they came to an old stone lodge on the inside of a forbidding iron gate. The ancient building was in a bad state of neglect. Tiles were missing from the roof, the leaded windows were broken and dirty, the little garden a mass of ugly weeds. Beyond the rear fence a narrow, grassy drive trailed out of sight into a distant plantation.

Victoria Lincoln pulled the car on to the grass verge and turned off the engine. Following her example, Carol slid from her seat, went with the detective across to the huge iron gates of the lodge.

Pushing them open, Victoria pointed to the gravel drive, through which weeds sprouted profusely. Carol caught in her breath sharply as she saw what had attracted Miss Lincoln's attention.

Faintly visible were the distinctive tyre marks of a motorcar!

'That's rather strange, isn't it, Vicky?' breathed Carol; formality had been dispensed with when the detective and her assistant were alone. 'I'd say no one's used this place in years — yet those marks were made not so long since . . . weren't they?'

Victoria nodded grimly.

'They were, Carol. See here, too.' She pointed to where, on one of the stout iron pillars of the gates, several deep scratches had been made. See where the paint's been chipped and scraped off — perhaps by a car mudguard, or bumper? Notice anything remarkable about these scratches, Carol?'

Her assistant bent to examine them. Then she nodded sharply.

'Why — they haven't even started to

get rusty yet! That means they weren't made so very long ago! Right, Vicky?'

'Bull's-eye, my dear! I really think we should take a look at this lodge.' She began to walk up the drive. 'Come on, Carol.'

Both front and back doors were locked securely. A little whistle from Carol, who was peering through one of the rear windows, brought Victoria hurrying to her side. Carol pointed to where a half-circle of dust had been scraped from the grimy floor.

'See that? That door's been opened recently. The dust has been shifted as it was pushed open!'

'You're right, Carol. And I'm pretty sure that if only we could get in there we'd find more evidence of this somewhat mysterious visitor!'

Victoria Lincoln sat silently behind the wheel as they drove back into Ashford. In the High Street she pulled up outside a chemist's.

'Won't be a minute, Carol. I want some lavender water.'

Carol remembered then that she needed toothpaste. It'd be too late for any shopping when they returned to London. She stepped out and followed Victoria into the shop.

At the counter the detective pointed to a display of large bottles with bright yellow labels.

'*Dr. Horace Potter's World Famous Seasick Remedy*,' said a printed card. '*Half price to clear — 2/6 per bottle.*'

The chemist nodded.

'Ah — there's no sale for that stuff now, ma'am. I'll be glad to get rid of it.'

'Really? And why has it stopped selling?' Victoria said, politely.

'Well, I only ever had one customer for it, but she bought it regularly. Lady Enid Carson, from Fellsgarth Manor. Terribly bad sailor, she was — every time she took a sea trip — which was pretty often — she came in for two or three bottles. Since she died,' — he shrugged — 'nobody ever asks for it. There's precious few folks in Ashford ever go to sea!'

Carol set her teeth suddenly and a little shiver ran up her spine. Sir Robert had stated very clearly that Lady Enid was a *good* sailor!

Back in the car she asked breathlessly, 'What does it mean, Vicky?'

'Just this, my dear: Sir Robert lied because he wanted us to believe his wife wasn't scared to go walking on deck during a storm. See? If he'd told the truth and said she was a *bad* sailor, then naturally we'd have asked: 'Well, why didn't she stay in her cabin'?'

'Then — then you think he's lying about everything else? You think Mary Reid is right — that Lady Enid never went on board at all?'

The detective's face was grim as she started the engine.

'I do, Carol. Nevertheless, we've a stiff job on to *prove* anything!'

They stopped again at the end of the High Street, this time at a garage, for petrol. Carol said: 'Supposing we try to find out if Sir Robert had any repairs done to his car shortly after his wife disappeared? I'm thinking of those scratches on the lodge gates. If they were made by *his* car, I bet his mudguards were dented. And — '

Miss Lincoln laughed encouragingly.

'Carol, my darling! You're getting positively — ' She paused. 'I've been thinking the same thing myself, matter of fact. Inside that lodge would be a marvellous place to hide a body . . . '

As she paid the attendant she said:

'Can you tell me which garage looks after Sir Robert Carson's car? Who does all his repairs and so on?'

'Why, we do, ma'am. We've done Sir Robert's work for years.'

A little overpayment worked wonders. Confidentially, Miss Lincoln said;

'I want to know if he had any repair done to his mudguards, or bumpers — say about three months ago? You'll have records in your books, won't you?'

They had. Nine weeks and four days ago, exactly, Sir Robert had brought his car in to have a bad dent in the offside front mudguard knocked out and repainted.

★ ★ ★

A few days later, as Sir Robert Carson sat at breakfast, the butler brought in the letters. Amongst them was a small flat parcel, the address typewritten.

Curiously, the baronet untied the string, lifted the lid of the slim box. Inside, on a tiny bed of cotton wool, lay a blue cameo ring. Sir Robert's florid cheeks paled as he stared at it. Enid had worn a ring just like this on the night she'd . . .

Feverishly he unfolded the single sheet of notepaper tucked beneath the cotton wool. It contained only a few typewritten lines:

Dear Bunty,

I must see you at once, but I dare not come to the house. I'm sending you my ring so that you'll know it really is me who's writing.

Will you meet me outside Ashford Station at ten o'clock Wednesday morning! I will explain everything then.

Enid.

The baronet shuddered as he gazed at the extraordinary epistle. A letter from the dead! That was Enid's signature all right, and it was her ring — and she'd called him by his nickname — Bunty. He stared wildly about the room. There seemed something unnatural about this — something *horrible* . . .

He took a gulp of hot coffee, realising suddenly that this was Wednesday. He jumped up, rang for Parkes, the butler, When the manservant appeared he said:

'Tell Thompson to bring the car round not later than nine-thirty, Parkes. I'm going into Ashford.'

'Very good, sir.'

The hands of the station clock stood at ten minutes to ten when Sir Robert jumped from his car, which he'd pulled up opposite the station entrance. He found that his heart was thumping wildly as be walked a little way up the street, and from a shop doorway turned to keep watch on the folks streaming in and out of the station portico.

Suddenly his hands clenched tightly and he started forward. From near the bookstall just inside the station yard he'd caught a glimpse of a tall, slim woman in a pale-green two-piece . . . the very suit Enid had worn on that hideous night when they'd set off for Calais . . .

He left the doorway, went slowly down the street, keeping close to the wall. His heart pounded so hard he couldn't even think clearly. If only that woman in green would turn round! If only he could see her face . . .

She didn't though. She crossed the yard at a tangent, came out of the street by the far exit. The baronet halted suddenly then as he saw her hat. There was no mistaking that elegant affair, with its black pillbox crown and sprightly green feather. He dodged into another doorway. Yes — that was Enid all right — see how her glossy dark hair fell in a bunch on her shoulders! She'd worn that hat, too, that night . . .

He thought it strange that she didn't stop on the pavement and wait; but no — without even glancing round she set off down the High Street. As if drawn by a magnet, Sir Robert followed, his breath coming in heaving gasps. He kept telling himself, out aloud, that this was a nightmare . . .

Suddenly the woman in green turned

left up a side street. He put on a spurt, lessening the distance between them. What on earth was Enid's game? Why hadn't she waited at the station?

He turned the corner just in time to see her pushing open the gate of a house and walking up the little path. It was right opposite a lamp post — impossible to mistake it . . .

He dashed forward, calling her name. Still she didn't turn. She was at the door now — she was opening it, passing through. In less than a minute he'd reached the house. Enid had left the door open . . . breathlessly he ran up the path. He caught a glimpse of her disappearing up the stairs as he flew into the hall.

Again he called her name. He could still see her, walking along the landing towards a door at the far end. A terrible shudder ran through him as again she made no sign that she'd heard him. The door opened. She went through, out of sight. He heard the faint click as the door closed . . .

He went up the stairs three at a time. The floorboards creaked and quivered as he raced down the landing. Next moment he'd flung the door open and was staring round in blank amazement.

The room was bare of furniture! A worn piece of lino covered the floor, but that was all. On his left an old woman in a dirty brown overall was rubbing a window with a duster. She turned round quickly as the baronet charged in, her grey, wrinkled face puckered in bewilderment.

Sir Robert gulped.

'Er — sorry, ma'am ... but I'm looking for the lady in green who just came in here. She's my wife — I want to speak to her. I — '

He paused. He felt like screaming, like tearing his hair out. Was he going mad? The old woman was staring at him, her mouth wide open, her thin fingers plucking fearfully at her lips.

'Woman in green, sir?' she quavered. 'Nay, you've come to the wrong house, sir, that you 'ave. I've been cleaning in here this last half-hour, and no one's been in, sir, I assure you. You try next door, sir — they let rooms off next door, too. Perhaps they — '

'Rubbish!' Sir Robert snapped viciously. 'D'you think I'm crazy? I tell you I saw her come in here — I followed her from the station . . . she came in here, through the hall, up the stairs — I was right behind her . . . I tell you, I actually saw her coming along this landing and go through the door! I heard the click as it closed!'

He went near, grabbed the old woman's shoulders.

'Where is she?' he roared. 'You tell me, or — '

She squirmed out of his grasp, darted to the door; but the baronet's bulky figure barred the way. She started to shout weakly.

'Help — help! You must be mad, sir! I tell you there's no one here . . . '

Sir Robert snarled helplessly. This old idiot couldn't help him, it seemed. He pointed across the room to a door in the far corner.

'Where does that lead to?' he demanded.

'Down to my kitchen, sir,' quavered the old woman. 'Have a look down there, sir, if you like . . . it's open . . . '

Sir Robert dashed over. Had Enid crept

through here without the old girl seeing or hearing her? But why? What on earth was she *playing* at?

He was chuckling foolishly as he pulled the door open. Much more of this ghastly business and he would be mad . . .

A flight of wooden stairs led to the floor below. He went down quickly, found himself in a cosy little kitchen. The door leading into the yard was ajar. He went out, through an alley and back into the street.

He couldn't stop himself trembling as, ten minutes later, he returned to his car and drove slowly out to Fellsgarth Manor.

★ ★ ★

Sir Robert Carson glided his car into the little lane that wound beyond the ancient lodge, stopped the engine and alighted. He fought hard against the crazy beating of his heart as he walked up the narrow, weed-grown drive. In his hand was a large, rusty, old-fashioned key. With this, he opened the back door.

He stepped into a low-roofed little

room, the principal feature of which was a deep, grateless fireplace. For a time the baronet stood gazing at this. Then he went softly over, scuffled the debris to one side with his foot, and bent to examine the joints of the big hearthstone.

Next second a peculiar sound left his lips — an exclamation in which terror and amazement were strangely mixed. He'd brought a heavy tyre lever with him from the car. Hurriedly, he put the claw of it into a crack and levered up the stone.

Raising himself, he threw all his weight on the lever, thrusting it farther and farther down. Presently the stone came up above the edge of the floor. Sir Robert kept it in that position by holding the lever taut with one hand. With the other, he gave the stone one terrific heave and hinged it up.

As he paused for a moment the loud rasp of his laboured breathing filled the silent little kitchen. Then he took out his torch and flashed its beam into the dark cavity.

'Oh, Heaven!' he shrieked.

He turned to rush from the room; but

apparently a miracle happened — for two burly men sprang from the shadows near the door and grabbed him.

Sir Robert Carson went back down the little drive escorted by two Ashford detectives, and with a pair of handcuffs gleaming on his wrists.

★ ★ ★

It was towards dusk on the following day that Miss Mary Reid again sat in Victoria Lincoln's office; this time, to hear the amazing story of the arrest of the baronet.

'To my mind, the whole thing hinged on whether Lady Enid was a good or a bad sailor,' the famous detective explained. 'If she'd been a bad one — which, of course, she was — she wouldn't have been on board that ship for fifteen minutes without calling for the stewardess. She didn't though — because, as you said, she never *was* on board!

'Sir Robert told everyone she was a good sailor because naturally he wanted folks to *believe* that she left their cabin to go strolling round the deck. It was our fortunate visit to the chemist that really started us on Sir Robert's trail. He'd told such an obvious lie about his wife that I knew he was trying to cover up something dreadful.

'So I paid a visit to Colonel Alvin Herman, Chief Constable at Ashford, and explained my suspicions. He lent me two of his best men and we went to the South Lodge on the Manor estate — for from what we'd discovered, I was certain Sir Robert had been there recently with the car.

'We picked the lock on the back door and entered. In the kitchen we found chips and cuts near the hearthstone, which showed it had been recently levered up. So we removed it — and beneath, we discovered the fully-clothed body of Lady Enid!'

Mary Reid sat bolt upright in her chair. Her face was white, her pale eyes fairly goggled.

'Good heavens!' she gasped. 'That horrible scoundrel had murdered her! I knew it all along! Oh, dear . . . to think that my poor Margaret might have met the same dreadful fate!'

Miss Lincoln nodded gravely.

'To continue, Miss Reid. Our problem now was to trap Sir Robert into giving himself away. If somehow he could be made to believe that Enid hadn't been completely dead when he'd buried her beneath the stone, that she'd actually escaped and was anxious to see him, perhaps . . . I felt sure he'd go back to the lodge to make sure whether her body *was* there or not.

'So, as I said, Lady Enid's body was removed, her green suit, black hair and cameo ring were handed to me. From a club membership card in one of her pockets I took a copy of her signature; and using the baronet's nickname which you'd learned from your sister, Miss Reid, I typed a little note to Sir Robert, asking him to meet his 'wife' outside Ashford Station yesterday morning.

'A detective was following him the whole time. I dressed in his wife's things — for, from your information, I knew Lady Enid and I were just about the same height. I waited behind the bookstall in the station yard. Outside, my assistant saw Sir Robert arrive and hurry off up the street, where, from a convenient doorway, she kept watch on the station entrance.

'She came and told me; and I, careful to keep my face turned away, strolled into the street and into a house not far away — an apartment house kept by the mother of a local policeman, who'd been very carefully rehearsed in the part she had to play.

'Foolish Sir Robert! He followed, saw me go into the house, up the stairs, into the room. He was only yards behind me all the time! Then I skipped down the back stairs and back into the street. The landlady denied all knowledge of me, as she'd been told to do.

'Now you can readily understand the result of all this. The baronet was simply scared out of his wits. He just couldn't understand what had happened — and the only way to settle the problem was to go to the lodge and see if Enid's body was there or not.

'This is exactly what he did. And the two detectives I had hiding arrested him after he'd levered up the stone. It was just as good as if he'd been actually caught in the act of murdering her. Inside the hour he'd made a full confession!'

Miss Mary Reid took a deep breath.

'What a supremely clever and brave woman you are, Miss Lincoln! I simply cannot express my gratitude and admiration in mere words.' She took out her cheque book. 'Will you name your fee, please, my dear?'

From her desk near the window Caroline Gerrard smiled softly to herself.

The amazing Victoria Lincoln had triumphed again!

THE END